The Out-of-this-World Adventures of
~~Tim~~ Tim ~~Timmy~~ Hunter

The **Mirror** of
DOOM

By Bailey Baxter
Illustrated by LaSablonnière

Mirror of Doom

Special thanks to Grace and Caleb Blanchard, Harrison Best, and all the readers of earlier versions of this novel.

Without your interest and encouragement, *The Mirror of Doom* would have stayed trapped in my overly active imagination.

And a big shout out to Hannah Krieger, editor extraordinaire, and proofreading genius Darran Hanson who helped make this book the best it could be.

Prologue

I felt like a complete loser.

My brother and sister could have been killed because of me — not to mention a dude named Gavril. He's a prince, but you wouldn't have heard of him.

Because of my stupidity, I put them all in danger. And where did I end up? Captured by an evil queen and locked in the top room of a stone tower like one of those dumb fairytale princesses.

It was humiliating.

To make matters worse, it was dark in the tower — so dark I couldn't even see my hand in front of my face. And drafty. Wolves were howling outside.

And I was probably going to die in the morning.

So how did a twelve-year-old kid from Connecticut get himself into such a mess?

It all started with my sister's diary...

Grandma's House

3rd floor is "off limits"

Creepy Uncle Edgar

Lulu

← football

My "cool" brother, Ron... on the phone with some girl...

My sister, Kat, writing in her stupid diary again

Me and some of my awesome action figures!

(This is one of my best drawings, it took me like 3 hours to do)

My Itchy Fingers

It really was Kat's fault.

None of this would have happened if she didn't leave her diary lying on the coffee table in our grandma's living room.

I mean... come on! How was I supposed to resist getting enough dirt on my bossy, fifteen-year-old sister to torment her for the rest of her life?

I'm only human, you know.

Besides, it was the perfect set-up. Mom was working the late shift at the grocery store. Grandma was at her quilting club. (It meets every Monday night.) Weird Uncle Edgar was hiding as usual on the third floor. And my brother and sister were watching a football game in the "TV room."

There was no one there to stop me.

I quickly glanced around — just to make sure I really was alone — and slipped the diary into the pocket of my cargo shorts.

Mission accomplished.

I headed toward the doorway, feeling quite proud of myself, and ran smack into Kat.

My heart stopped.

"Watch where you're going, Timmy," she said, pushing by me with a toss of her long, dark hair.

My heart started up again and began pounding in my ears. I braced myself for the worst. She was going to kill me. Dead. And it was going to hurt.

But then I remembered. She didn't know I had her diary. I took a deep breath. I was safe. I just had to act casual — and innocent.

"I thought you were watching the game," I said, leaning (casually) against the door frame.

"I was. But I came to get my—" Kat stopped and stiffened as she looked at the empty spot on the coffee table. Her head slowly swiveled toward me.

"Timmy..."

Uh-oh!

I started backing out of the room. "Can't talk now. I have to let the dog out."

"Give me back my diary!"

Kat lunged for me, but I dodged her outstretched arm and took off down the hallway with a screech of my Nikes.

"Get back here, you little runt!"

I darted through the dining room and startled Grandma's poodle Lulu into one of her yapping fits. I jumped over the dog and made for the front stairs, scrambling up them two at a time. Pausing to catch my breath on the second floor landing, I turned to see Kat standing at the bottom of the stairs.

How did she do that so fast?

"Timmy, I want my diary back. Now!"

Not a chance.

I whipped around, flew up the next set of stairs, and screeched to a stop on the third floor.

The *forbidden* third floor.

When our mom moved us into Grandma's old Victorian house, we were told that we were not allowed up there — under any circumstances.

I looked around, wondering what the big deal was. It certainly wasn't a place I'd want to hang out.

The hallway was long, gloomy, and full of dark shadows. The wallpaper was peeling, cobwebs were dangling, and faded photographs of long-dead relatives hung crooked on the walls.

If Uncle Edgar lived up there like my grandma said he did, he was even weirder than I thought.

Hesitantly, I started down the "Hall of Terror." (Trust me, that was the perfect name for it.) I peeked into several of the rooms as I passed — and became totally convinced that Grandma had hired the Addams family to decorate.

Everything looked so old, broken, and creepy. And there was no sign of Uncle Edgar anywhere, which made me nervous. I had only seen the guy once or twice since we moved in, but he's not someone you want popping out at you in a dark, spooky place.

Or anywhere, for that matter.

The hallway ended at a closed door. I hesitated, staring at it. Its glass doorknob sparkled in the dim light, inviting me to turn it.

"Timmy!"

I spun around to face my archenemy. Batman had the Joker. Spiderman had Venom.

And I had Kat.

She was standing at the top of the stairs. Her arms were crossed, and she was scowling. I didn't have to be an expert at reading body language to know she was totally ticked off.

"Where is it, Timmy?"

"Where's what?" I shoved my hands into my pockets and tried to look innocent. I felt the familiar hard case of my PlayStation in one pocket, and its presence was somehow comforting. In the other pocket, of course, was...

"My diary!" Kat shouted again, her nostrils flaring. I had never seen her so mad, but I wasn't going to be scared into giving up my prize that easily.

"What makes you think I have your stupid diary?"

Kat turned and yelled down the stairs: "Ron, get up here."

Uh-oh. Our brother Ron was sixteen and the star quarterback of his high school football team. He regularly bench-pressed more than my weight — with his pinky finger. If Ron sided with Kat like he usually did, he would be bench-pressing *me* next.

Ron appeared at the top of the stairs in two seconds flat. And he wasn't even breathing hard. "Make it quick, Kat," he said. "The game's tied, and I don't want to miss anything."

"Timmy took my diary, and I want it back."

Ron's eyebrows shot up, and he looked slightly impressed. "Really? Wow, the kid has more guts than I thought."

Kat's hands flew to her hips. "Ron!"

"Take it easy. I'm on it."

Ron started down the hallway toward me. "Timmy, give Kat her diary back, or I'll take it from you myself."

He would, too. But I wasn't about to give him the chance.

I turned and threw myself against that mysterious closed door, giving the glass knob a big twist. It opened suddenly, and I found myself stumbling forward into a dark room. Quickly regaining my balance, I shoved the door closed. It took a bit of fumbling in the darkness, but I found the key and quickly turned it.

Locked. And just in time, too.

The doorknob jiggled.

"Timmy, open this door," Ron said.

"Nope."

Ron's fist slammed into the other side of the door with a loud bang. "Open the door, runt!"

"Go away. I've got some reading to do."

"Timmy!" Kat practically screamed my name through the door. "If you even open my diary, I will kill you. Do you understand?"

Oh, I understood all right. But come on! Kat's diary was usually guarded more closely than Fort Knox. This could be my ONLY opportunity to see what's inside. I'd be crazy NOT to read it!

I slid the little book out of my pocket and stretched out my other hand to feel for a light switch — and froze, my heart pounding. I heard a noise. It sounded like a footstep.

And it seemed to come from *inside* the room.

"Timmy, open this door!"

"Kat, just shut up for a minute!"

Surprisingly, she listened. I strained my ears, hoping and praying I was wrong about that footstep. Nope, there it was again — and this time it was *closer.*

There was someone else in the room!

Dropping the diary, I frantically groped for the doorknob with both hands. "Help! Get me out of here!"

I heard Ron sigh. "Timmy, stop fooling around and just open the door."

"I'm trying!"

I found the doorknob and gave it a twist.

"The doorknob won't turn! Why won't it turn?"

Then it came to me.

I had locked the door!

I had locked myself into a strange, dark room with a crazed killer — or worse!

Stupid! Stupid! STUPID!

"Timmy, enough of your games. Open this door now!"

"Kat, I'm trying!"

Sliding my suddenly clammy hands over the door, I desperately felt for the key. Floorboards creaked eerily behind me again and again as someone — or something — crept closer.

"No, please no," I whispered.

I had seen enough commercials for horror movies to know that bad things happen to kids that wander into dark places.

Really bad.

And I wasn't ready to die yet, thank you very much.

Suddenly, a light flicked on.

I clung to the door and flung my arm up to shield my head from the oncoming blow.

A Close Encounter of the Creepy Kind

It didn't come.

After a few long moments, I began to feel ridiculous. I slowly lowered my arm and turned around. What I saw was shocking.

I was looking at a room so messy it would have given my mom a heart attack. The drawn curtains were crooked, the bed was unmade and piled high with dirty clothes and used dishes, and the floor was covered with wobbly stacks of books and papers. An empty cage that might have once been home to a gerbil or guinea pig was perched on the only chair.

It was so different than the first two floors of my grandma's house — where she daily tackled invisible specks of dust with the help of a battered feather duster and a wheezy old vacuum cleaner. It didn't look like Grandma had visited this room with her trusty cleaning tools. Ever.

Then I saw the man.

He was standing by an old-fashioned floor lamp, stroking his goatee, and staring at me. He had piercing, coal-black eyes and bushy eyebrows that resembled two large, furry caterpillars.

"Uncle Edgar!"

My mother's only brother frowned at me. "What

do you think you're doing in here?"

"Uh, sorry. I didn't realize... I mean... is this your room?"

"Of course it is. What else could it be?"

"Then why was it so dark in here? You could keep some lights on, you know. You scared me half to death."

Uncle Edgar came toward me, reminding me of a cheetah stalking a defenseless antelope.

And guess who the antelope was.

"You are supposed to stay off the third floor," he said.

"Yeah, I know. But my sister and brother chased me up here."

Ron chose that moment to pound on the door again. "Timmy, open up!"

"Or I'm telling Mom, Timmy," Kat said. "And you'll be grounded. Did you hear me? Grounded!"

I cocked my thumb toward the commotion. "See?"

A gleam came into Uncle Edgar's eyes. "Does your grandmother know you're here?"

"Of course she does, remember? She invited us to live here when Erick disappeared. Mom couldn't afford the rent on our house any more without the money he made with his carpentry business."

(Erick is our stepdad. He vanished without a word two months ago.)

"That's not what I meant, you idiot!"

With a glance at the door, where a lot of noise was still coming from Ron and Kat, Uncle Edgar drew in close to me. Uncomfortably close.

"Does your grandmother know you're on *my* floor? In *my* room?"

He smelled like a combination of Fritos and lavender. I quickly shuffled back and found myself against the door again.

"Uh, no. She's at her quilting club."

Uncle Edgar took another step forward. "And your mother? Where might she be?"

"At work."

He leaned in closer, his nose almost touching mine. "So no one knows you're in here, besides those two noisy people outside the door?"

"Uh, I guess not," I said, trying to answer while holding my breath.

To my relief, Uncle Edgar stepped back. He stared at me, stroking his goatee. "Really? That's very interesting."

Kat jiggled the doorknob. "Timmy, come out here now! I want my diary back!"

"Her diary?" Uncle Edgar's eyes shot to my hands and, when he saw they were empty, traveled to the floor. There was no mistaking the look on his face when he spotted Kat's most prized possession just lying there.

"No! Don't—"

But I was too late. Before those two tiny words were even out of my mouth, Uncle Edgar had pounced on the diary like a monkey on a cupcake.

I grabbed for it. "Hey, give it back!"

Stepping quickly away from me, Uncle Edgar examined the diary's cover in the light. "So you're running from your sister. I can see why."

"Look, it's not what you think. I was bored, so I took it. But I didn't mean any harm."

Those furry eyebrows went up again. "I'll bet *she* means *you* some harm."

I couldn't help but glance toward the door where the pounding and shouting continued. "Yeah, no kidding. Can I have the diary back, please? Kat is mad enough."

"Not until I show you something."

Uncle Edgar grabbed my wrist and started pulling me across the room.

"Hey! What's the big idea? Let me go!"

I tried to break free, but the crazy old coot was a lot stronger than he looked. He and Ron should arm wrestle. Uncle Edgar would probably win.

It only took a couple of seconds to reach the opposite side of the room, but it felt like years. Uncle Edgar stopped in front of a tall object shrouded in a sheet and finally dropped my arm.

"Ta da!" he said, gesturing widely.

Now that I was free, I wanted nothing more than to put some distance between Uncle Edgar and myself — even if it meant facing Kat. But I couldn't help but be curious.

"What is it?"

With a gleam in his dark eyes, Uncle Edgar gave the sheet a tug. It slid off to reveal a full-length mirror.

I'm normally not interested in mirrors. In fact, Kat has told me many times that it would do me good to look into one once in a while. But this mirror was really something.

It had a fancy golden frame that was covered with carved pictures of trees, animals, and mythical creatures I'd only read about in books.

And I had seen it before.

"Hey, that's Erick's mirror!"

"It's beautiful, isn't it?" Uncle Edgar said. "It's a

genuine antique, dating back to the 1700s. Maybe even earlier. Rumor has it that it belonged to the Grimm family."

"Yeah, well it doesn't any more. It belongs to my stepdad. What are *you* doing with it?"

Uncle Edgar ignored my question. "Look into the mirror, boy. What do you see?"

"But it's not yours. You need to give it back."

"Look into the mirror!"

Reluctantly, I obeyed, expecting to see a scrawny twelve-year-old boy with dark, spiky hair (thanks to a headful of cowlicks) and skinny white legs.

That's what I always saw — which is the reason why I stayed away from mirrors. But this time was different.

"I'm not there! I have no reflection!"

"That's right."

I looked at Uncle Edgar. "How did you make my reflection disappear? Are you a magician or something?"

Uncle Edgar reached out and stroked the mirror gently with his hand. He was looking at it the same way Ron looks at pretty girls.

Ick! The guy definitely had a few screws loose.

"I didn't do anything, dear boy," Uncle Edgar said. "This mirror just happens to be a doorway into another world."

I couldn't help but laugh. "Yeah, sure it is. And the carpet we're standing on flies!"

"Don't be ridiculous." Uncle Edgar moved behind me and put his hands on my shoulders. It was a fatherly gesture, but it felt all wrong coming from him.

"Just look into the mirror again," he said. "You

would expect to see this room, right? But it's not there."

I hated to admit it, but Uncle Edgar was right. The bedroom wasn't reflected in the mirror at all. In its place, I saw rough stone walls, a plain wooden bench, and part of an old tapestry hanging on the wall.

"Well, it does look like a different room. But that doesn't prove anything."

"Then look here." Uncle Edgar pointed to the words carved into the mirror's frame. They began at the bottom left corner and ran throughout the other designs on the frame like a road winds through mountains. He began to read:

> *"When the moon from the sky doth flee*
> *The door in the glass shalt open to thee.*
> *A new world beckons, but thou shalt learn*
> *That without courage thou shalt not return."*

I frowned. "I don't get it."

Uncle Edgar threw his hands up. "How can you be so stupid? Don't they teach you anything in school? This isn't exactly rocket science, my boy."

"Well, no, but —"

Uncle Edgar went smoothly on, as if I hadn't said a word: "It's as clear as day. The poem says that when the moon disappears from the sky, the door in the mirror is open."

"Okay..."

"And when does the moon disappear from the sky?"

He waited expectantly for my answer.

"In the morning?"

Uncle Edgar looked like he wanted to smack me. "No! When it's a new moon! Like we have right now."

"I see," I said, but I didn't. And there was no fooling my wacky uncle.

"Maybe you need a demonstration." He flicked his wrist and something flew from his hand. It gave off a soft blaze of light as it made contact with the mirror, and then it disappeared.

"Wow!" I drew close to the mirror to look. Sure enough, a small book was now lying on the previously empty floor. The words on its cover said "My Diary."

My Diary?!

I felt all the blood drain from my face.

"You... look what you..." I sputtered. "Look what you've done! You threw my sister's diary into another world!"

"Ha! You *do* believe me!"

The pounding on the door grew louder. "Timmy, what's going on in there? I want my diary back!"

"I think you have a problem, young man," Uncle Edgar said.

"Thanks to you! If Kat kills me, it'll be your fault!"

Uncle Edgar held up both hands. "Hey, watch where you're throwing the blame, kid. You shouldn't have taken the diary in the first place."

I sighed. Uncle Edgar had a point — sort of. "What am I going to do?"

"Go after it."

"What? Are you crazy? I can't go to another world."

Uncle Edgar looked down and poked at a pile of books with the toe of his shoe. "Nothing to it."

"So you've done it before?"

"No, but I tossed a guinea pig through the mirror once, and it scurried off just fine."

"What? You threw a guinea pig into another world?"

Uncle Edgar's eyes snapped up. "That's what they're for, aren't they? They're guinea pigs."

"You're crazy! I should report you to the animal rights people!"

Uncle Edgar draped an arm around my shoulders. "Look, my boy, it's no big deal. Just stay on this side of the mirror and reach through for the diary. It should be perfectly safe."

"*Should* be?" I shrugged away from his arm. "No way, man!"

But then I heard Kat speaking to Ron in the hallway: "Go grab the key from that other door. Maybe it will open this one."

Uncle Edgar chuckled. "She's coming for you, boy."

"What? Are you saying that other key will open *this* door?"

"Of course it will. That's how it works in these old houses. One key fits all."

I threw up my hands. "That's it. I'm dead."

"Just get the diary back, and then your troubles will be over."

"Are you sure it's safe?"

"Perfectly."

Don't think for one moment that I trusted shifty old Uncle Edgar. But what was I supposed to do? Wait for Kat to burst into the room so I could explain to her that her precious diary was in another world?

No way. My odds of survival were better if I just got the diary back.

Taking a deep breath, I crouched in front of the mirror. Uncle Edgar was standing right beside me. Too close, again. That guy seriously had no concept of personal space.

"Go ahead," he said. "Reach for it."

Reluctantly, I stretched my arm out toward the mirror. I felt a slight tingling as my hand touched the surface and pushed through. It was so weird to see it on the other side of the glass.

I kept reaching. Soon most of my arm was through the mirror, but I still couldn't touch the diary.

"Keep going," Uncle Edgar said. There was a strange excitement in his voice.

I could hear the key turning in the lock. Kat and Ron would be in the room at any second.

With a sense of desperation, I pressed my shoulder through the mirror. Stretching my arm out as far as it could reach, I could just brush the diary with the tips of my fingers. I almost had it.

And then the worst things imaginable happened all at once.

The door flew open.

Kat yelled my name.

And I went sprawling head first through the mirror.

Pushed! Uncle Edgar pushed me!

I picked myself up off the hard wooden floor and looked around, stunned.

I was in a large, round room with very high ceilings. Sunlight streamed through long, narrow windows, revealing gray stone walls covered with tapestries, a big fireplace stained with soot, and one very plain bench. A tall, fancy mirror stood in the shadows.

The mirror!

I raced over to it — and stopped. A boy with dark spiky hair and skinny legs was staring back at me, fresh scrapes on his bony elbows and knees.

"Oh, no!" I said, sinking down to the floor.

The boy in the mirror did the same.

I reached out a shaky hand and felt the cool, hard surface.

It was solid, just like a normal mirror.

There was no way back.

Stuck

I don't have to tell you that things looked bad.

Very, very bad.

I was ALONE in another world! Anything could be lurking out there — *anything*!

Like dragons. Yeah, knowing my luck, this place was loaded with them.

And they all probably ate boys like me for lunch.

I'd be deader than a squashed spider — and no one would even know what happened to me.

I paced the floor, mad at Uncle Edgar for pushing me, and even madder at myself for falling for his dirty trick.

What if I never got home? What if I ended up stuck in another world forever? Would anyone even care?

Yeah, Mom and Grandma might shed a tear or two. But Ron and Kat? Knowing them, they were high-fiving each other, giving "thank you" hugs to Uncle Edgar, and doing Rock-Paper-Scissors to see who gets my Star Wars action figures.

If only I hadn't grabbed Kat's diary in the first place!

I looked over at where it was still lying on the floor.

"This is all your fault," I told it.

The strange thing was, now that I had the diary

all to myself, I didn't even feel like reading it. I had more important things to do.

Like getting back home.

I glanced around the room, hoping to spot Uncle Edgar's guinea pig. It would have been nice to have some company while I came up with a plan. But I didn't see it anywhere.

With a disappointed sigh, I went to one of the windows to look out — and discovered something that made me forget all about the guinea pig.

I was at the top of some kind of tower! How cool was that?

There was no glass in the window, so I was able to lean out for a good look. The tower stood tall, stretching higher than the tree tops. It was connected on both sides to huge stone walls and surrounded by a wide trench of water.

I pushed away from the window, thinking. My tower was at the corner of a much larger building, so there had to be other people around. Maybe they could help me get home. Or, at the very least, feed me.

I had to go find them!

Dashing over to the door, I gripped the big iron ring that served as a handle. I started to tug but then stopped, my blood turning colder than a Popsicle.

Something was scratching on the other side of the door!

I dropped my hand from the door and listened. Could it be the guinea pig?

Then I heard sniffing and a loud growl.

Nope, too big. WAY too big!

I backed away from the door.

"Go away!" I yelled.

The sound of my voice whipped whatever-it-was into a frenzy of scratching and snarls. I watched in horror as the door shook under its attack.

The creature was going to break through! It was going to tear me into bite-sized pieces and eat me like an order of "Timmy McNuggets"!

I had to protect myself. I looked around frantically for something — *anything* — I could use as a weapon.

And found nothing.

"What is wrong with you people?" I asked out loud. "Would it kill you to hang a bazooka over the fireplace?"

I was dead. That's it. Dead.

I sank to the floor and covered my face with my hands as silence settled in around me.

Silence?

I lifted my head and strained my ears. I couldn't hear the creature any more.

Did it leave?

I crept closer to the door, listening.

"Timmy?"

I nearly jumped out of my Nikes. Whipping around, I saw someone standing in front of the mirror — *on this side!*

"Ron!" I ran to him and almost knocked him over with a big bear hug. "You came!"

Ron seemed surprised by the hug, but he acted glad to see me anyway. "Are you okay?"

"Yeah, but I scraped up my knees a little."

"Man, we were worried about you. Uncle Edgar said if we didn't come after you, you'd be eaten by a dragon or something. Why did you go through the mirror? That had to be the stupidest thing you've ever done."

"But Ron, I didn't —"

And that's as far as I got. My explanation was interrupted by my sister's arrival — and she wasted no time greeting me.

"There you are, you little runt!" she said, charging at me with fire in her eyes.

I quickly ducked behind Ron.

"This is the stupidest thing you've ever done," Kat said, circling Ron. "Taking my diary was bad enough, Timmy. But going to another world? What were you thinking? I was worried sick."

She was worried? Maybe she *did* care! But she wasn't done yet.

"You're an idiot, Timmy, you know that? An idiot! Just wait until Mom hears about this. She'll ground you for life!"

She was in my face now. I stepped back.

"But I didn't want to go through the mirror, Kat. Didn't you see what happened? Uncle Edgar pushed me!"

"No. All we saw was Uncle Edgar standing in front of the mirror," Kat said, frowning. "Why would he push you?"

"I don't know. Maybe he ran out of guinea pigs. The guy's a loony toon, Kat!"

"Well, that doesn't mean you're off the hook, Timmy." Kat snatched up her diary from the floor and shook it at me. "If you ever touch my stuff again..."

"...I'm dead meat," I said, finishing her sentence for her. "Yeah, I know."

"Okay, fine. Let's go home."

"We can't."

Kat stared at me like I had suddenly grown two heads. "What do you mean we can't?"

"The mirror isn't working."

"Of course it's working." Kat walked over to the mirror with me trotting along behind her. "I just came through it."

"I know, but look." I pressed my finger against the glass. "It's solid. And we can see our reflections. It's acting like a regular mirror."

Ron crowded in between us. "It's got to work. Maybe there's a reset switch."

Kat rolled her eyes. "It's not a computer, Ron!"

"Then what are we supposed to do?"

"I don't know!" Kat began to pace the room. "Just shut up and let me think."

"Well, you'd better think fast because I need to get back," Ron said. "I've got a date with Tammy on Friday night."

"The cheerleader?" I asked.

"The *head* cheerleader." Ron sighed. "She's beautiful, man. I can't stand her up. Kat, you've got to do something!"

"What am I supposed to do, Ron? The mirror isn't working!"

"That's what I told you," I said.

Kat turned on me. "And you be quiet, Timmy. It's your fault we're all in this mess."

"It's Uncle Edgar's fault. He's the one who pushed me."

"No, it's *your* fault. You're the one who stole my diary."

"Yeah, but you should have known better than to leave it out where I could see it. So, technically, it's *your* fault."

Kat fumed. "Timmy, don't even go there."

Ron stepped between us and pushed us apart. "Will you two just stop it? This isn't helping us get home."

"Well, if you have any ideas," Kat said. "I'd be glad to hear them."

"We could read the poem," I said.

Kat's head jerked around so fast I was certain she gave herself whiplash. "What poem?"

I pointed at the mirror. A poem was woven throughout the design on the frame — just like it was on the mirror in Uncle Edgar's room.

Frankly, I felt a little foolish that I didn't notice it earlier.

Ron pushed me out of the way. "Let me see." He began to read out loud:

> "The door in the glass shalt open to thee
> If thou art shown brave to be.
> A heroic deed shalt allow thee to pass.
> Cowards seeth merely a looking glass."

Then he scratched his head. "What's *that* supposed to mean?"

"It's simple," Kat said (in a "know-it-all" tone, I might add). "We just have to do something brave before we can go home."

"Really?" Ron looked relieved. "No problem. We'll save a baby from a runaway train and be home in time for supper."

Kat made a scoffing noise. "And where do you think you're going to find a train around here? This place looks practically medieval."

"Oh."

I thought for a moment. "Hey Ron, maybe we can find a damsel in distress to rescue instead!"

Ron's eyes lit up. "Good idea, Timmy! But, she's got to be beautiful."

"You've got to be kidding me," Kat said.

"Well, do you have any better ideas?" Ron asked.

Kat shook her head. "Let's just get out of here. The sooner we find something heroic to do, the sooner we can go home."

She approached the door and reached for the iron handle.

"NO!"

I dashed around my sister and threw myself in front of the door, arms outspread.

"Timmy, get out of my way. What is wrong with you?"

"There's some kind of creature out there!"

Kat and Ron stared at me for a moment — and then burst into laughter.

Yes, *both* of them.

I felt my cheeks get warm. "Go ahead and laugh, but I've been hearing strange noises."

"Like the ones the monsters make under your bed?"

"Ha, ha. Very funny, Kat. I'm not kidding. There's something big and scary out there."

Ron shoved me aside and put his ear against the door.

"Ron, don't humor him."

Ron put up his hand. "Shush, Kat. I'm listening." After a couple of moments, he shook his head. "I don't hear a thing."

"See, Timmy?" Kat said. "There's nothing out

there."

Despite my protests, she reached around Ron and pulled open the door. It screeched loudly, making me jump. We cautiously stepped out onto the landing of a steep spiral staircase made entirely of stone.

I gave a little cry. "Claw marks, see? Look at the claw marks on the door!"

Kat barely glanced at them. "It's an old door, Timmy. Of course it has a few scratches."

"Not scratches. *Claw marks!*"

"Timmy, enough! There is no creature, okay? Your little joke is over!"

"But it's not a joke, Kat! I swear it!"

"I mean it, Timmy. Stop it! I don't want to hear anything more about your stupid creature!"

Kat turned with a toss of her head and started down the stairs. Ron gave me a sympathetic shrug and followed her. And I was left standing there, my finger still pointing at the deep gouges in the door.

Do you see what I have to put up with?

I sighed and started down the stairs after Ron and Kat. What else could I do? Stay alone up in that room with that creature prowling around? Not a chance of that happening.

We stopped briefly at the next landing to inspect the room there and discovered it looked exactly like the one we had just left. Only, it didn't have a mirror.

We passed one more landing — with one more nearly identical room — before we finally reached the bottom.

Pushing open a heavy, wooden door, we found ourselves in a large courtyard. Its gray stone walls were anchored in each corner by a tall tower. And in the center stood a huge, sparkling black stone.

"Wow," I said. "We're in a castle!"

"It seems to be abandoned," Kat said, moving forward in the thigh-high grass. "It doesn't look like anyone has taken care of the grounds in a long time."

Ron grinned. "Cool! If no one's here, we can explore!"

"NO!"

The word came out of my mouth before I could stop it, but come on! We were in an abandoned castle with a deranged creature lurking nearby. And Ron wanted to play tourist?

Had he completely lost his mind?

Kat's hands flew to her hips. "What's your problem, Timmy?"

"I just want to get out of here!" *Before we're torn to pieces*, I added to myself.

"Right, forget about looking around," Ron said with a grin. "We need to find that damsel in distress. Where is the way out?"

Kat pointed at a tall, boxy tower that stood in the middle of one of the walls. An arched opening was cut through its center.

"We go that way — through the castle gate."

Ron shook his head. "I don't know how you know this stuff."

"Easy. I watch *The History Channel* instead of *ESPN*."

"Yeah, whatever."

"Guys, shut up." I said, holding up my hand. "I heard something."

"Timmy, I told you! I don't want to hear another word about that—"

Kat stopped in mid-sentence as a loud growl

filled the courtyard. The expression on her face was classic.

"What on earth was that?"

I pointed across the courtyard. "Look!"

Something large and dark was moving toward us through the tall grass — and it definitely *wasn't* the guinea pig.

Kat screamed. "Run!"

Surrounded

Ron bolted for the gate, and I'm not ashamed to say that Kat and I were close behind him.

Heroic? Not exactly. But if you had heard that growl, you wouldn't have stuck around either.

Ron reached the gate first, clattered across the drawbridge that stretched over the trench of water (make that moat), and raced across an open field.

Remember how I said he plays football at his high school? Well, he also runs track. Yep. By the time Kat and I reached the drawbridge, he had vanished into the woods on the far side of the field.

I glanced back over my shoulder into the courtyard. The creature was still headed our way — and I swear I caught a glimpse of its fangs.

"Faster, Kat! It's coming!"

Kat gave a little squeal and picked up the pace. Yeah, she ran like a girl — with her elbows flapping like wings by her sides — but she burned through the field and up the forest trail like an Olympic runner.

I normally would have had trouble keeping up with her. But on that day, my legs were turbocharged.

It's amazing how fast you can run when you're scared. We even caught up with Ron.

It was then that the forest turned against us.

The trail grew even narrower — if that was possible. Low branches grabbed at us as we ran by, and tree roots tried to trip us up. The underbrush got so thick that I wasn't even sure we were on the trail any more.

"I see a clearing up ahead," Ron shouted. "Come on!"

Ron crashed through the bushes with Kat right behind him. I looked down for just one second to get untangled from a prickly vine, and when I looked up, they were gone.

"Ron!" I shouted. "Kat?"

I couldn't believe I was alone — again!

I ran ahead, frantic. Branches were pulling at my clothes and scratching me up something awful. If I had known I would be running through a forest to escape being eaten alive by some scary creature, I would have worn jeans instead of shorts.

With a fresh burst of energy, I tore through a clump of evergreens — and plowed right into Kat.

What happened next was a blur, and it most definitely was *not* my fault.

Kat and Ron were standing at the top of a steep hill. When I bumped into Kat, she bumped into Ron, and we went barreling down the hill in a cloud of dust.

After flattening nearly every bush on the slope, we landed in a bruised heap at the bottom.

I was lucky. I ended up on top of the pile.

"Get off me!" Kat shoved me aside and rolled off of Ron.

Ron groaned and made no move to get up. "Tell me that didn't just happen."

"Hey, are you okay, man?" I asked, reaching

down to help him.

Ron ignored my hand and pushed himself up on his own. "Timmy, when are you going to learn to watch where you're going?"

"I was trying to catch up with you. What were you and Kat doing standing at the top of a steep hill like that anyway?"

"Trying to find a safe way down."

"Oh. Sorry."

Kat suddenly gasped and looked up the slope. "Oh, no!"

"What is it?" Ron asked, on instant alert. "Do you see the creature?"

"No, I lost my diary. I dropped it when we fell."

I couldn't help but laugh. "You go all the way to another world to get your diary back, and you lose it within like five minutes? That's perfect!"

"Oh, shut up. If you didn't run smack into us, we wouldn't have fallen. And I wouldn't have lost my diary!"

"It was an accident! I'm sorry, okay?"

"Sure you are. Now, thanks to you, I need to climb back up there and try to find it."

"That's dumb," I said. "In case you've forgotten, there's a big, scary creature after us — and I'm sure it wants to *eat* us. We need to keep moving, Kat."

Kat shook her head. "I have to find my diary. It's personal. What if someone else picks it up?"

"Hello?" I gestured widely with my arms. "We're in the middle of nowhere. Who's going to find it? A pack of coyotes? They can't *read!*"

"I wouldn't expect you to understand, Timmy. Now, get out of my way." Kat pushed me aside — quite roughly, I might add — and started up the slope.

"Wait!" Ron said. "I just heard something."

Kat scrambled back down the hill toward us, her precious diary apparently forgotten.

"The creature?" she asked.

"I don't know. Just shut up and listen."

I huddled close to Ron and Kat, suddenly aware of the thick cluster of trees that crowded around our little clearing. I could hear the sound of birds calling to each other high up in the branches and the whisper of the breeze moving through the leaves. But the forest around us was too dark and full of shadows for me to see much of anything.

Ron moved a shaking hand toward his pocket and pulled out a Swiss Army knife.

Kat's eyes grew wide. "Ron, what are you doing?"

"If that creature attacks, we need to have a weapon to fight it," he said, using his fingernails to pry out the largest blade.

"You couldn't fight a turnip with that thing!" Kat said. "Just put it away before someone gets hurt!"

"No way. I've got this."

"Shhh!" I said. "What was that?"

Ron and Kat shushed quickly — and the rustling sound I thought I heard was unmistakable.

Something was definitely out there.

A nearby branch swayed wildly. Kat gave a little whimper and grabbed Ron's arm as a gray shape leapt into the clearing.

Kat screamed. Ron dropped his pocketknife. And then I began to laugh.

"A squirrel! It's just a little squirrel!"

"What a relief," Ron said, snatching up his knife and pocketing it. "For a moment, I thought it was the creature."

Kat nodded. "I did, too." She paused, scanning the shadowy forest around us. "I wonder where it is."

"Me too," I said. "It should have attacked us by now and torn us to shreds."

Kat gave her signature eye roll. "Not helping, Timmy."

"Maybe we lost the creature when Timmy pushed us down that hill," Ron said.

"I didn't push. I bumped."

"Whatever," Kat said. "But the sooner we get out of here, the better. So let's just keep moving."

She struck out on the trail which led deeper into the forest, with Ron just a few paces behind her.

I followed along, straining my eyes for any sign of the creature. But it was useless. With the thick leaves blocking out most of the sunlight — and a tangled mass of brambles, bushes, and vines covering the ground — the creature could be hiding nearby with five of his closest, hungriest friends, and we'd be none the wiser.

Kat stopped suddenly, a stranger-than-usual expression on her face.

"What's going on?"

She shushed me — and then I heard it.

A loud rustling noise, followed by the snapping of a twig.

My heart did a backflip. Something was moving in the woods again!

Oh, please be a squirrel. Please be a squirrel.

Another twig snapped.

Not a squirrel! Too big!

"It's the creature!" I whispered.

Kat clutched at Ron's arm. "Your knife! Get out your knife!"

The leaves crackled on the other side of us. Kat gasped. I clung to Ron's shirt like a frightened five-year-old.

Suddenly, the shadows came to life. Dark forms leapt out of the underbrush on both sides of the trail.

Kat screamed (again).

Ron whipped out his pocketknife (again), but he actually managed to hold on to it that time.

Not that it mattered much. What good is a Swiss Army knife when you're surrounded by a group of guys holding swords?

Yeah, you read that right. *Swords*.

"Stay close," Ron said to us, rather unnecessarily. Kat and I were already clinging to him like lint on a sweater.

As the men drew nearer to us, I noticed they were armed with more than just swords. Some of them held spears, and several carried bows and arrows. Their Robin Hood-style tunics and pants were dirty and torn, and a few of the guys wore makeshift bandages.

They all seemed very interested in Ron's pocketknife.

One man stepped away from the others. He was tall with shaggy blonde hair. He didn't look much older than Ron, but he seemed to be the one in charge.

"Drop your weapon!"

Ron instantly obeyed, closing the blade and allowing the pocketknife to drop with a soft thump to the ground. The leader scooped it up, examined it briefly, and slipped it into a pouch on his belt.

Ron cleared his throat. "Uh, we don't want any trouble, okay?"

The leader took a moment to look us over. He had the hardest, coldest gray eyes I've ever seen.

"Do you know where you are?"

Ron looked at me and Kat, his eyes wide. He obviously did not know the answer to that question — but neither did we.

Ron cleared his throat. "Uh, not really. We're new here, and we're kind of lost."

Mr. Leader Dude stepped closer, the point of his sword inches from Ron's chest. "You're in the forest of Fenimore."

Ron backed up a step. Kat and I went with him.

"Fenimore? Okay, thanks. Good to know. Can you point us to the nearest town?"

As if on some unseen cue, the men raised their weapons in one synchronized movement and pointed them at us. It would have been cool if it wasn't so terrifying.

"You don't seem to understand," the leader said. "You are *trespassing* in the forest of Fenimore. Now, tell me what you are doing here."

"I've already told you," Ron said. "We're lost."

"Yeah," I said. "We're lost."

The leader frowned. "Do you really expect me to believe you?"

Ron nodded. "Sure, it's the truth."

"It's the truth," I said.

"Timmy, stop that," Kat hissed.

"Stop what?"

"That stupid echo."

"What stupid echo?"

The leader ignored me and Kat. His unwavering gaze was on Ron. "Who are you?"

Ron blinked and looked surprised. He probably wasn't expecting such an easy question. "Uh, I'm Ron Hunter. This is my sister Kat and that's my brother Timmy."

I raised my hand. "Actually, it's Tim. Not Timmy."

Ron and Kat stared at me.

"Well, it is! I'm twelve now, you know."

"I don't care if you're Goldilocks," the leader said, still only speaking to Ron. "Perhaps a better question would be: *What* are you?"

Ron scratched his head. "What?"

"Exactly."

Ron just stared at him. He opened his mouth, but no words came out.

"So you have no answer for me."

Ron scratched his head again and tried a tactic that usually worked like a charm for him in school: "Can you repeat the question?"

"Allow me to answer the question for you." Mr. Leader took a step forward, his gray eyes blazing. "You are spies, sent by the queen."

My mouth dropped open. "You think we're from England?"

"We're not spies," Kat said quickly.

"Perhaps not," the leader said. "But you have not given me a reasonable explanation as to why we've found you so near to Fenimore Castle. So I must assume you *are* spies."

He raised his sword.

"And for that, you must die."

The Forest of Fenimore

Dudes dressed like "Merry Men"... but not at all "merry"

sword

pocket Knife

Huge, scary guy

The Leader

Ron being brave

Kat

Me hiding behind my sister (not my most heroic moment)

Prisoners

At the sight of a dozen swords raised to strike, I screamed — yes, screamed — and dove behind Ron.

Please do not point out the fact that it would have been a great time to do something heroic so I could go home. I don't want to hear it.

Kat wasn't any braver than I was. She gave a scream of her own and also tried to hide behind Ron. It took a bit of elbowing and scuffling for both of us to fit.

Poor Ron had nowhere to go. He threw up his hands in the universal sign for surrender and squeaked — yes, squeaked — "Whoa, wait a minute!"

He cleared his throat and tried again in a more normal voice: "We're not spies. We came here through a mirror from a different world!"

The men didn't back off, but Ron's comment did get them to exchange glances and mumble to one another.

"Nice move, Ron," I said. "Now they think we're spies *and* crazy."

The leader was frowning. "You came here through a mirror?"

"The prophecy!" a tall man with a bushy beard said. "We're saved!"

The leader gave him a look. "Cyril, that's

enough." He turned back to Ron and repeated his question: "Did you really come here through a mirror?"

"Yeah," Ron said. "It was in our Uncle Edgar's room. He pushed Timmy through and then Kat and I followed. We ended up in an old abandoned castle not far from here."

"Fenimore Castle," the leader said.

Ron shrugged. "Well, I don't know the name of the place. It wasn't like there was a sign or anything."

The leader sighed and sheathed his sword, motioning to his men to do the same. I swear he looked disappointed.

"This changes things. We won't kill you — yet."

"Thanks," I said. "That's real nice of you."

Yeah, I was being sarcastic. But come on, the guy wanted to kill us just because he suspected us of being spies. *Suspected* us! What did he do to jaywalkers? Boil them in oil?

Fortunately, the leader dude didn't pick up on my tone of voice. In fact, he didn't pay any attention to me at all.

"You didn't see anyone else at the castle?" the leader asked Ron.

"No. It looked like no one has lived there in ages."

"No one has. That's why we chose it as our rendezvous point."

"The king should have arrived some time ago, my lord," said a rough-looking guy with a surprisingly high-pitched voice. "He left Tryton with his party before we did."

"Yes, I know. Perhaps he took the longer route."

"What should we do?" the man asked.

"We go to the castle as planned and wait for him." The leader then turned to Ron. "You and the others will have to accompany us."

"But what about the creature?" Kat asked.

The leader looked surprised. "What creature?"

"There was a creature at the castle," Ron said.

"It was huge," I said. "And black. With really big, sharp teeth."

"Sounds like a galrog, my lord," Cyril said.

"What's a galrog?" I asked.

"It's part animal, part devil," the leader said. "It has the strength and speed of a panther and the intelligence of a wolf. Its fangs tear through flesh as easily as a knife cuts through butter."

I blinked. "Wow, I'm sorry I asked."

The leader towered over me. "And if you really were close enough to see its 'big, sharp teeth,' you'd be dead right now."

I gulped. "Are you serious?"

"I'm always serious."

"But it followed us into the forest," Kat said. "What if we run into it?"

"Then we will deal with it. Now, get moving."

We got moving.

As we retraced our steps back to the castle, I started to forget that we were practically prisoners of a Robin Hood wannabe that would like nothing better than to see us hanged as spies.

And I began to actually enjoy myself.

It was such a perfect day for a hike. The sun was shining. The leaves overhead gave us some nice, cool shade. Birds were singing, squirrels were chattering, and the bugs weren't bothering me like they usually do when I'm outside.

It was peaceful, calm, and, yes, even beautiful in the woods. So it was easy to overlook a certain grumpy leader and his crazy spy theories.

Unfortunately, the peace and quiet didn't last long.

"GALROG!"

A galrog? *For real?*

The warning had come from some guy at the end of the line. I whipped around, trying to see past Ron and Kat.

Now, don't get me wrong: I didn't *want* to see a galrog. I was hoping that it was all just a practical joke to scare the new kids in town. (That would be us.)

The leader pushed past us with several of his men, sword in hand. "Stay here," he said as he rushed by.

And there went my practical joke theory.

Ron and Kat appeared no more eager to meet a galrog than I was, so we huddled together and watched as the men warily approached a cluster of bushes a stone's throw from the trail.

The branches heaved wildly, drawing a shout from the men and a gasp from Kat.

The archers let their arrows fly.

The bushes were still.

A heavy silence filled the forest. Not even the birds were chirping.

I held my breath as the men cautiously approached the bushes and used their swords to push back the branches.

"It's gone!" one of the men said.

It was my turn to gasp. "Are you kidding me?

43

How could you guys miss something as big as that? You were right on top of it."

The leader sheathed his sword and marched over to me. "Perhaps next time, we'll let *you* have a go at it. Alone."

Silence fell again in the woods. This time, it was just plain awkward.

Then one of the men laughed. "That little runt up against a galrog? Now that would be a sight to see. I'd be willing to wager he can't even lift up a sword, much less use one!"

The other men laughed. Ron and Kat joined in, which didn't surprise me at all.

Personally, I didn't think it was the least bit funny.

The only one *not* laughing at me was the leader. He actually looked worried.

"Something's not right. Why didn't the galrog attack?"

"You're upset the galrog *didn't* attack?" Kat asked around her giggles.

Yeah, she was still laughing at me. Some sister, huh?

"They always attack," the leader said. "Unless..."

"Unless what?" I asked.

"Unless it was tracking us." He paused and looked at me, Kat, and Ron. "Or you."

A Ridiculous Prophecy

Mr. Leader's theory about the galrog sent little shivers up and down my spine. I was hoping he was wrong. I'd rather not have a scary, demonic creature following me around, thank you very much.

But at least he got Kat to stop laughing.

"It probably was the same galrog that followed us from the castle," she said. "But why would it be tracking us?"

The leader shook his head and changed the subject. "Let's move on. The sooner we reach the castle, the better."

I followed along without a word of protest. I just wanted to get out of those woods — and fast.

What if we met another galrog? Would they really make me fight it? I'd be toast if they did. You know I would.

Thankfully, the rest of our journey back to the castle was quick and galrog-free. But I couldn't rest until I was safely inside. So, I practically flew across the sagging drawbridge, hurried through the gate, and then stopped, amazed.

The empty, seemingly abandoned courtyard we had left on the run was now filled with about three dozen men. Some were tending to their horses. Others were hanging out and talking. And quite a few of them were getting their wounds bandaged.

Their *wounds?*

"Where did all these people come from?" I asked, running to catch up with the leader. "And what happened to them?"

"The king has arrived," he said, looking relieved. "You three wait by Dragon Rock."

"Dragon Rock?" I asked.

The leader sighed and pointed at the big rock in the center of the courtyard. "There." He turned to Cyril. "Watch them."

Then he headed with some of his men across the courtyard and disappeared through a huge, nail-studded door. Cyril took up his position near us, his hand resting on the hilt of his sword.

I swear he was looking for trouble, so we played it safe and didn't give him any. But that didn't stop Kat from complaining.

"This is a fine mess you got us in, Timmy."

"It's Tim. Not Timmy."

"We can't afford to be stuck here in the castle, *Timmy*," Kat said. "We need to find something brave to do, so we can go home. Mom is probably already worried sick about us."

"Well maybe you should tell that to the grumpy leader dude, Kat. He's the one who brought us back here. Not me."

"Well, we wouldn't even be here in the first place if you didn't take my diary — which I've lost forever, thanks to you."

"Enough about your stupid diary, already! I wish I never laid eyes on the thing."

"Me too!" Kat said.

"Okay. Whatever." Ready to be done with the argument, I leaned back against the big, black rock —

and quickly changed my mind.

"Ouch! This rock is hard!"

Kat burst out laughing. "Of course, it's hard, Timmy! It's a rock!"

"But it's the hardest rock I've ever felt. Look at those clear veins in it. They're like glass or something. Maybe that's why they call it Dragon Rock. Maybe it's special."

Kat shook her head. "Maybe you're an idiot."

"Am not!"

"Are too!"

"Will you two just shut up?" Ron said.

A strange man had approached while we were arguing. "You three, come with me."

That shut us up.

With nervous glances at one another, we silently followed the man across the courtyard and through the big, heavy door we saw the leader use earlier.

And then everything went dark.

You know how it is when you go from bright sunshine into a dimly-lit room? Yeah, I couldn't see a thing at first.

But when my eyes adjusted — *Wow!*

The first thing I noticed was the fireplace. It would be hard to miss because it stretched out over one-third of the wall. The ginormous shield that hung over it looked way too large for one man to lift — much less fight with. It was either made for a giant or just for decoration. (Just between you and me, I was hoping my "giant" theory was wrong.)

The walls were covered with tapestries, and someone had spread a bunch of straw on the floor, like the place was a barn or something. (Later, I learned the straw was called "thresh" and was meant to make the cold stone floor warmer to walk on.)

The room was large, but it seemed filled up by the long table that stretched down the center of it. Seated around it in uncomfortable-looking high-backed chairs was a group of men.

They all looked very serious.

The leader was standing next to the man seated at the head of the table in the biggest, grandest, most uncomfortable-looking chair of them all.

"These are the three I told you about," he said to the man in the fancy chair.

The man stood and walked toward us. He was dressed much like the other men. His gray-streaked brown hair and beard were neatly trimmed. A slim band of gold sat upon his head with a large bluish gem of some kind in the center.

The man who had led us into the room gave me a little shove. "Bow to King Gunther of Tryton."

King?!

We quickly obeyed with some of the most awkward bows these guys have ever seen.

How do I know we did so badly?

The men's faces had that contorted "I'm trying not to laugh" look. And one guy actually did laugh out loud, but he covered it up by pretending to cough.

"Welcome to Fenimore Castle," King Gunther said in a friendly tone. His gray eyes crinkled at the corners as he smiled at us. "Gavril says you came here through the mirror in the south tower."

That struck me as strange. The king seemed so casual about it — like people were always dropping in through the mirror for a spot of tea or something.

"We did," Kat answered him. "But who's

Gavril?"

The king looked surprised. "He's the one who found you in the forest and brought you back here."

We all stared at the leader, who was standing beside the king. I figured he had a name, but *Gavril*? Really? He looked more like a Brutus if you ask me.

"He didn't introduce himself," Kat said.

"Well then, I'll have to fix that." He gestured grandly. "I'd like you to meet Gavril, my son."

"Your son?" I squeaked.

"Wow," said Ron. I swear I could see the wheels turning in his head. "If he's your son, then he's a—"

"Prince," Kat said, finishing his sentence for him. "So I assume we call you Prince Gavril?"

Gavril cleared his throat and looked away. "Just Gavril is fine. I'm not prince of anything anymore, thanks to Morissa."

King Gunther clapped a hand on his shoulder. "Son, all is not lost. Don't forget about the prophecy."

Gavril pulled away from him. "You *should* forget that so-called prophecy, Father. It's just an old wives' tale. Besides, look at them. How can they help us? They're just children."

"Hey, I'm not a child," Ron said, looking offended.

"Me neither," I said, although obviously I was. I just didn't want them *thinking* I was.

"What's this prophecy you people keep talking about?" Kat asked.

The king looked at his son. "Gavril, you tell them."

Gavril pursed his lips together, looking like he'd rather swallow a bag of needles. Finally, he sighed.

"It's an old rhyme:

> *"When evil through the land does spread*
> *And darkness fills young and old with dread*
> *Hope will come when least looked for,*
> *Through a mirror as through a door.*
> *Behold the three from a distant land*
> *Against them evil cannot withstand."*

Ron shrugged. "Nice poem. But I don't see what that's got to do with us."

"Don't you see?" King Gunther said. "You came through the mirror. You're the three from a distant land."

Ron frowned. "So?"

"You are the ones we've been waiting for. The great warriors who will finally defeat the evil queen."

Meeting the King

Big uncomfort-
able chair

The Leader,
Mr. "Poker Face"

The very serious
looking King

cool stuff

51

Blackmail

What was our reaction to King Gunther's big announcement?

Stunned silence. You could hear crickets chirp.

Then Ron, Kat, and I looked at each other and burst out laughing. We couldn't help it. It was the most ridiculous thing we had ever heard.

Great warriors? *Us?*

The king needed a major reality check!

"I think you've confused us with someone else," Kat said, when she managed to stop laughing.

"Yeah, we're not warriors," Ron said. "We're kids, for Pete's sake."

Gavril jumped all over that. "I thought you said you *weren't* kids."

"You know what I mean," Ron shot back.

King Gunther held up his hands. "Maybe I exaggerated a little when I called you great warriors. But I know you are the three from the prophecy. You have been sent here to help us defeat the queen."

"I wasn't sent here," I said. "I was pushed."

"This is crazy," Kat said. "How are we supposed to defeat a queen?"

The king smiled. "It's simple. You just have to go to the castle in Tryton, retrieve a certain mirror, and bring it here to me."

"You're sending them to Tryton?" Gavril asked.

"After what just happened there?"

"*What* just happened there?" Kat asked quickly.

You can't get much past my sister.

King Gunther shook his head. "Gavril, that's enough."

"Father, we were ambushed by the queen's soldiers. I lost some of my best men!"

"She was expecting us, Gavril. She won't be expecting these three."

"She will be now," Gavril said, sounding a bit reluctant to admit it. "One of her galrogs was tracking them."

The king's eyebrows shot up. Obviously, that was big news.

"You didn't kill it?"

"We tried, of course. It slipped away."

The king sighed and made a little gesture. Two of the men sprang up from the table and scooted his big chair over to him. He heavily sat down in it and rubbed his forehead.

"Will someone please tell us what's going on?" Kat asked.

"We've run into a little trouble in Tryton," the king said. "Queen Morissa has used her considerable charms to bewitch the soldiers there and has taken over my kingdom. The only way to stop her is to destroy her mirror."

"I don't get it," I said. "What does her mirror have to do with anything?"

"It's magic."

"Okay..."

The king pushed himself out of his fancy chair and began to pace. "The mirror gives Morissa her power. It allows her to see whatever her enemies are doing. All she has to do is ask the right questions and secret meetings like this one, troop movements, and ambushes are all revealed to her."

"That's right," Gavril said. "And she can use that information to conquer kingdoms and expand her rule. That's why the mirror must be destroyed."

Kat was frowning. "Okay, let me be sure I have this straight. You want us to steal a magic mirror from the queen so we can go home through a *different* magic mirror?"

The king nodded. "Yes, that is correct."

"How many magic mirrors do you people have?"

King Gunther stared at her. "I only know of these two. Why? Don't you have magic mirrors in your world?

Kat's left eyebrow flew up. "Apparently. Or we wouldn't be here."

Gavril gave a little snort. Either he was holding back a laugh, or he had accidentally swallowed a bug. Hard to tell for sure.

The king shot him a look and cleared his throat before answering Kat. "Oh yes, of course."

"Well, I don't see why the queen's mirror needs to be brought back to you." Kat said. "Why don't you just have someone like Gavril sneak into her castle and break it? End of problem."

Gavril also cleared his throat. "It's not that easy. According to my father, there's only one substance hard enough to destroy the mirror."

"Dragon Rock," King Gunther said. "Our folklore says that a dragon once breathed fire on that rock during a great battle hundreds of years ago and crystallized it — making it the hardest substance in our world."

"Ha! I told you that rock was special!" I said to Kat.

She gave a little huff and rolled her eyes.

"Yes, it's very special," the king said. "That's why I need you to bring the mirror back here. To me."

"But it's magic," Kat said. "She'll see us coming. We won't stand a chance."

"Nonsense. She won't suspect you're coming, so she won't even think to ask the mirror about you."

"She might, Father," Gavril said. "You're forgetting about the galrog."

The king dismissed his words with a wave of his hand. "How can a galrog tell her anything? It can't talk. Besides, I believe *you* are forgetting about the *prophecy*."

Gavril threw his hands up. "Yes, I'd very much like to forget all about that prophecy!"

"Me too!" Kat said. "I don't care what you people say, but there's no way we're doing this. It's too risky. Surely there's some other brave thing we can do to get home."

The king made a tsk-tsk noise. "Retrieving this magic mirror won't be nearly as hard as you think."

"But there's no way we can succeed! We don't know where the queen's castle is. We don't know how to find the mirror once we get there. We don't even know what the thing looks like!"

I found myself nodding my head. For once, I agreed with Kat.

"That's why I'm sending Gavril with you," the king said. "He'll help you."

Gavril's head whipped around. "Father, you

must be joking! You're sending me into Tryton with these three idiots?"

"Hey, who are you calling an idiot?" Ron said.

Gavril glanced at him. "No offense."

King Gunther put a hand on Gavril's arm. "Son, the only way to save Tryton is to get that mirror. I know these three are the ones of which the prophecy speaks. They can deliver us."

Gavril shrugged off his hand. "You can't be serious about this. Have you *looked* at them? They're not capable of delivering us from anything!"

True. I wouldn't trust the three of us to deliver a pizza.

"Don't worry, Gavril," Kat said. "We're not going to do it. We're not going to get ourselves killed over something as dumb as a mirror."

The king blinked. "So you won't go with Gavril?"

"How many times do I have to tell you?" Kat said. "No, we're not going!"

The room suddenly fell quiet. The king stared for a long moment at Kat and then turned to Gavril.

"You found these three trespassing in the forest of Fenimore, is that correct?"

Gavril sighed. "Yes, father."

"They are probably spies sent by the queen," the king said. He turned to his men who were hovering nearby. "Take these three to the dungeon to await trial and execution."

My jaw must have dropped all the way to the floor. It was like watching David Banner turn into the Incredible Hulk — except the supposedly nice king turned mean, not green.

Strong arms grabbed us and began pulling us

toward the door.

"You can't do this to us!" I shouted as I got dragged along. "We're not spies! We were lost!"

King Gunther put up his hand. The men stopped.

"Bring me the queen's mirror, and I'll drop the charges against you. It's the dungeon or Tryton. You choose."

Kat glared at him. "That's blackmail!"

The king shrugged. "Call it what you will. The choice is up to you."

"Can the three of us talk about it?" Kat asked. "In private?"

"By all means," the king said, sitting back down in his chair. "Take your time."

The men released us, and we scurried over to a quiet corner of the room.

"I don't see what we need to talk about, Kat," Ron said. "Sounds like a no brainer to me."

"You *want* to go to Tryton?"

Ron shrugged. "Sure beats rotting in a dungeon and being executed."

"If they kill us, I doubt we'll have *time* to rot in the dungeon, Ron," I said.

"Not helping, Timmy," Kat said.

"Look this isn't that big a deal," Ron said. "We need to do something heroic to get home anyway. And taking that mirror away from the queen would be better than fighting a dragon or something."

I nodded my head. "Ron's right. We should do it."

"It could also get us killed," Kat said.

I paused and began shaking my head instead. "Kat's right. We shouldn't do it."

"That Gavril dude will protect us," Ron said. "We sneak into the castle, grab the mirror, and sneak out. Piece of cake."

I found myself nodding my head again. Ron had a good point. Besides, he mentioned cake, and I was hungry.

"That's enough discussion," the king bellowed from his chair. "What's your decision? The dungeon or Tryton?"

Kat hesitated, looking at me and Ron. The room grew very quiet; so quiet you could hear rustling noises in the straw.

(Probably mice, if you're wondering.)

Someone coughed and cleared his throat.

"Well?" the king asked.

Kat finally turned to him.

"Tryton."

Night Hike

It was dark by the time we got started.

Yeah, I know it makes no sense to start a journey at night. I tried to tell Gavril we should wait until morning. Ron and Kat even agreed with me for once. But did Gavril listen?

Nope.

Surprised?

Me neither. Mr. Bad Attitude just wanted to get the whole thing over with, if you ask me.

Not that walking at night didn't have its benefits. It was nice and cool. And I didn't have to worry about getting sunburned. There was that.

But I couldn't see where I was going. I kept tripping over tree roots and snagging my backpack on branches in the dark.

Well, backpack may be the wrong word, since there was no "pack" involved — just a blanket wrapped around some dried food and tied with a rope. Yes, I was carrying it on my back, but does that make it a "backpack"?

It was a big nuisance; that's what it was. If it contained something useful — like a flashlight — I wouldn't have minded so much.

It didn't, of course.

I stopped and squinted up the dark trail, suddenly worried. "Which way did Gavril go?"

Squinting didn't help. The dark and the moonlight were playing tricks with my eyes. All I could see were a bunch of shifting shadows and the black, looming shapes of trees and bushes.

I really needed that flashlight.

"There he is," Kat said, pointing ahead. "He just passed through that patch of moonlight."

"Gavril!" Ron shouted, moving forward more quickly. "Wait up! Are you trying to lose us?"

"I wouldn't be surprised," Kat said in a low voice.

I hurried to keep up with her. "Do you really think he's trying to lose us?"

Kat just shook her head and kept walking, but that was enough to get me worrying.

What if Gavril planned to "accidentally" get separated from us? He'd be off the hook.

I could just imagine him telling the king: *I tried to take them to Tryton, Father. But those fools got themselves lost. They've probably been eaten by a herd of galrogs by now.*

Yeah, maybe I was getting paranoid, but you would, too, if you were being led through some strange woods in the dark by a guy who didn't like you.

To Gavril's credit, he did pause and let us catch up to him — somewhat reluctantly, I imagined.

"You've got to keep up," he said.

"We're not the ones who chose to travel by night, Gavril," Kat said. "That was your idea, remember?"

"Yeah," Ron said. "It would be a lot easier to follow you if we could see where we're going."

"We went over this already at the castle," Gavril

said. "I wanted to get in a few hours of marching before we sleep."

"Marching?" Kat sounded ticked off. "We're not soldiers, you know."

"Obviously."

"Thanks a lot," Ron said.

"Look," Gavril said, "I don't like this any better than you do. If you ask me, this mission was doomed from the start."

I sighed. Mr. Doom-and-Gloom was at it again.

"You have no idea of what we're up against," he continued. "The queen is very evil and very powerful. I should be storming the castle with a troop of the king's best soldiers. Instead, I'm stuck with you three."

"Look," Kat said. "This isn't our idea of a good time either. Why don't you just take us back to the king? We'll figure out another way to get home."

"No. The king believes you are the ones in the prophecy. I must follow his orders and take you to Tryton, whether I agree with him or not."

"Hey, the king's okay," Ron said. "He returned my pocketknife."

"He made Gavril return it, you mean," Kat muttered.

"Ron, how can you be thinking about that little pocketknife when the king gave the two of us swords?" I asked. "Real swords!"

"Now that was a mistake," Kat said.

I ignored her and drew my sword out of its sheath, enjoying the sound of metal sliding against metal and the cool weight of the weapon in my hand.

It was dark, but somehow Kat knew what I was up to. "Put that thing away, Timmy, or you'll put someone's eye out."

"Relax. It's not like I haven't handled one of these babies before."

Kat scoffed. "Dueling with plastic light sabers with your buddy Ben did not prepare you to use a real sword! I wouldn't even trust you with a butter knife!"

"Well, the king gave you a bow and some arrows, and you don't know how to use them either."

"I do, too! I took archery in gym class!"

"Yeah, well that doesn't exactly make you William Tell!"

"Enough!" Gavril said. "Must you two fight all the time?"

"We don't fight all the time," Kat said.

"Yeah, sis," Ron said, "you pretty much do."

"Well, if Timmy wasn't such a jerk—"

"Stop it!" Gavril sounded totally exasperated. "You two make more noise than a herd of elephants. Do you want to bring a galrog down on us?"

The answer to that question would be a big, fat "no," but I wisely kept my mouth shut. I didn't want to do anything to encourage one of those things to come around.

If anything, Gavril's words made me even more paranoid than I already was. As we continued walking (in silence), I realized that we still sounded very much like a herd of elephants as we crashed through the underbrush. I found myself listening to every crackle and rustle in the forest and wondering if a galrog was preparing to pounce.

I have to admit I was relieved several hours later when Gavril finally halted in the middle of a small clearing.

"Are we stopping?"

"Yes, Tim," Gavril said, "it is time we got some sleep."

Ron eased the pack off his back and stretched. "Great. I couldn't walk another step."

"Are we going to light a fire?" I asked. "Nothing like a fire when you're camping out."

"And there is nothing like a fire to keep the wild animals away," Gavril said, pulling a bundle of sticks off his back. "That's why I brought some kindling with us."

"Wild animals?" Kat asked.

"Yeah, those galrog things," I said.

Gavril bent his head and worked to untie the rope around the sticks. "Well, I was thinking of bears and wolves. Galrogs aren't deterred by fire."

"Really?" I said. "Are you serious?"

Gavril glanced up. "I'm always serious."

Looking at his stern, unreadable face in the dim light of the moon, I found myself believing him.

"Maybe you just need a vacation," I said. "Have you ever taken a holiday, Gavril?"

"I can't budge this knot. I'm going to need to cut the rope," Gavril said, *not* answering my question.

I swear he did it on purpose just to irritate me.

Ron fumbled in his pocket. "Gavril, do you want to use my knife?"

"No need." Gavril pulled a long dagger out of a sheath attached to his belt.

I couldn't help but gasp. It literally flashed in the moonlight. It was like seeing Luke Skywalker wield his lightsaber for the first time.

Ron pushed me aside. "That's some knife! Can I see it?"

With an annoyed sigh, Gavril held out the dagger.

I leaned over Ron's shoulder to get a closer look, and I wasn't disappointed.

The blade was long and deadly-looking, and the hilt — well, that was the best part. It appeared to be made of gold and was embedded with dozens of jewels.

It was the coolest (and most dangerous-looking) knife I'd ever seen.

"Wow!" I said. "Are those real diamonds and rubies?"

Ron gave a low whistle. "That's really something! It makes my Swiss Army knife look like a toy!"

Even Kat couldn't resist a look. "Gavril, where did you get a knife like that?"

Gavril quickly cut the rope around the kindling and slipped the dagger back into its sheath. "My mother gave it to me when I was just a boy — right before she died."

"Oh," Kat said after an awkward pause. "I'm sorry."

"Your mom had a knife like that?" I asked. "How awesome is that? Our mom only carries pepper spray."

"It actually belonged to my grandfather," Gavril said as he pulled apart the bundle of sticks. "The blade is silver, but it was tempered in such a way to make it incredibly strong. Rumor has it that my grandfather killed a dragon with it."

"Our stepdad has a cool knife, too," I said. "Only it doesn't have any jewels on it."

"Timmy, that's just an old hunting knife," Kat said.

"Yeah, but it's cool. He let me hold it one time — just a few days before he disappeared."

"Took off, you mean," Ron said, getting to his feet.

Gavril looked up from arranging the sticks into a mini teepee. "Your father disappeared?"

"No," Kat said. "Our father was killed in a car accident when we were really little. It was our mom's second husband Erick that just vanished without a word a couple months ago."

"Erick?"

"Yeah," Kat said, picking up a stick and studying it. "Erick Hunter. He was married to our mom for two years. He even adopted us. I don't know why he left. Maybe he met another woman."

"I think aliens got him," I said.

"That's stupid," Kat said.

"It is not. He was happy with us. He never would have left us on purpose."

Ron gave a sigh. "Do we have to talk about this? Let's just get the fire built before we're attacked by wild animals or something."

"I can help you, Gavril," I said. "I learned to make teepee fires in the Boy Scouts."

"I can manage. Ron, do you think you can see well enough to find some larger branches for the fire?"

While Ron went to scrounge up some firewood, Kat gave me a look. "Timmy, you were never in the Boy Scouts."

"My friend Joey was, so it's the same thing. He taught me everything I know about survival in the wilderness."

Kat laughed. "What you know about surviving in the wilderness could fit in a thimble."

"Ha, ha. Very funny."

"I think we had better get this fire going," Gavril said. "These dry pine needles should work well as tinder."

Gavril set a clump of pine needles onto a curved piece of tree bark and fished two stones out of his pack. Crouching over the tinder, Gavril struck the two stones together.

Ron picked that moment to come back. He dropped an armload of branches on the ground and stared at Gavril. "What are you doing?"

"I'm starting a fire," Gavril said, looking at him like he was a moron.

"With stones?"

"Not just stones. Flint and marcasite. They make the best spark."

"Why don't you use matches?"

Kat laughed. "Ron, they don't have matches here."

"Well, I have some." Ron drew a book of matches from the pocket of his shorts.

Kat's jaw dropped. "Since when do you carry matches?"

Ron shrugged. "I dunno. I found them yesterday on the kitchen floor and thought they might come in handy." He paused and grinned. "Guess I was right."

"What are you people talking about?" Gavril asked.

"Instant fire. Check this out, Gavril."

Ron struck a match and it flared into a flame.

Gavril leapt to his feet and scrambled a safe distance away. "What magic is this? That little stick ignited all by itself!"

I laughed. "It's just a match!"

Gavril crept closer and watched as Ron held the flame to the tinder and slid the burning needles into place under Gavril's carefully stacked sticks.

"Unbelievable," Gavril said, crouching down next to Ron. "Can I examine one of those, uh, matches?"

Ron handed the matchbook to him. "Just fold the cover over and strike the match on that rough strip."

Gavril followed his instructions and gave a laugh as the match flared in his hand. "Amazing! I've never seen anything like this before!"

"Man, you must be living in the dark ages," I said.

"Timmy," Kat said. "Don't be rude."

"What did I say?"

"No, he's right." Gavril tossed aside the spent match. "Thanks to the queen, we're living in very dark times indeed."

I studied his expression in the firelight, but ol' Poker Face was back. Too bad. For a moment there, Gavril had seemed almost human.

"We should get some sleep," Gavril said. "We have to get an early start in the morning."

Ron yawned. "Great idea. I'm tired from all that hiking."

"Marching," Kat said.

"Whatever." Ron stretched out on the ground near the fire.

"I'll take first watch," Gavril said. "Ron, I'll wake you up in a little while to take over for me. Then the others can take a turn."

Ron propped himself up on his elbows. "What are we supposed to be watching for?"

"Galrogs. And whatever you do, keep the fire going."

Ron plopped back down on the ground again. "Okay, no problem," he mumbled, already half-asleep.

I lay down on the ground, but my eyes refused to close.

What if a galrog found us?

If I was going to be attacked by one of those things, I wanted to at least see it coming.

Or did I?

An owl hooted overhead.

Somewhere nearby, a branch snapped.

I knew I was in for a long night.

A Cry for Help

My eyes snapped open.

The darkness had lifted, and a haze hung in the air. It was early morning by the look of it.

Sometime during the night, I must have fallen asleep. That was a nice surprise. With all the scary rustling and creaking noises coming out of the dark woods, I didn't think I would sleep at all.

Sitting up, I yawned, stretched, and looked around.

Kat was curled up next to the smoldering embers of last night's fire, Ron was snoring nearby, and Gavril was lying flat on his back, his hands folded neatly on his chest.

They were all still asleep — at least, I thought they were. (With Gavril, it was hard to be sure of anything.)

But hey! The fire was out. Wasn't someone supposed to keep it going?

I stood up to investigate and accidentally stepped on a twig, which made a loud snap.

Gavril instantly leapt to his feet with a sword in his hand and a yell on his lips.

I jumped about ten feet straight up into the air and gave a (scared) yell of my own.

Kat groaned and sat up, rubbing the sleep from her eyes. "What's going on?"

"Nothing," Gavril said, sheathing his sword. "Tim startled me, that's all."

"I was just checking the fire."

Gavril's eyes took in the smoking ashes, and his face grew grimmer than usual. "The fire is out. I told you three that it was vitally important to keep it going. Who was the last one on watch?"

Kat got to her feet and stretched. "Not me. No one woke me up to take over."

"Don't look at me," I said.

We all looked at Ron, who was still snoring peacefully.

Gavril walked over to him. "Ron, wake up."

No response.

Gavril nudged him with his foot and spoke more loudly: "Ron, get up!"

"Just ten more minutes, Mom," Ron mumbled.

Gavril looked at me and Kat.

We both shrugged. Ron was harder to wake up than Rip Van Winkle. Our mom has to use an air horn to get him out of bed in time for school every morning.

(Grandma's dog hates it.)

Gavril leaned down so that his mouth was right above Ron's ear. "Get up!" he shouted.

Ron sat up suddenly, banging his head into Gavril's face.

"Ow!" they both said.

I burst out laughing. I knew I shouldn't, but I just couldn't help myself.

Ron rubbed the side of his head. "Now what did you do that for?" he asked Gavril.

Gavril was holding his nose. He carefully removed his hand and checked for bleeding. There was none.

"Are you okay?" Kat asked him.

Gavril ignored her, his attention on Ron. "You let the fire go out."

"What?" Ron looked at the pitiful pile of ashes. "Oh, yeah. Sorry."

"Sorry?" Gavril towered over him. "That fire was supposed to protect us. We could have been attacked by wild animals in our sleep and killed!"

"Were we?" Ron asked, scratching his stomach and looking around.

"Were we what?"

"Killed. In our sleep."

"Well, no," Gavril said, sounding reluctant to admit that we weren't all mauled to death during the night. "Just don't let it happen again."

Then he turned and started rummaging through his pack.

"So, what's for breakfast?" I asked, artfully changing the subject. "I sure could go for a stack of pancakes with butter and maple syrup and some bacon on the side."

Gavril tossed me a piece of dried, salted meat. "Here you go."

I caught it before it hit the forest floor. "Hey, this is what we ate last night before we set out. What is this stuff, anyway?"

"Dried venison."

"Huh?"

"Dried deer meat," Kat said, biting into her piece.

"We're eating Bambi?"

"Get over it, Timmy," Ron said, pulling on his pack. "From the looks of it, this and some dried fruit are all we've got to eat."

Great.

"Let's get going," Gavril said. He swung his pack onto his back with one easy motion and struck out into the underbrush.

The hike was better than I expected — thanks to Gavril's ability to pick out a trail where there didn't seem to be one. The underbrush, which fought us every step of the way the day before, was parting before us like the Red Sea did for Moses.

But Gavril was quite a slave driver. He only allowed us one quick break for lunch — yeah, that deer jerky stuff again — and then we were off again. I had never walked so much before in my life.

"Are we almost there yet?" Ron asked.

"We have some distance to go," Gavril said. "We've been skirting Mount Kern, which is part of a larger mountain range. Eventually, we'll come to a pass that will allow us to cross over. The castle of Tryton is on the other side."

"Eventually?" I asked. "How long are we talking here? Hours? Days? Weeks?"

Gavril stopped suddenly and crouched down on the ground. "Be quiet!" he whispered, motioning us down.

We quickly obeyed.

"What's going on?" Ron whispered back.

"I heard voices up ahead. We may have trouble."

We stayed still and listened for a moment.

"I don't hear anything," I finally said,

straightening up.

"Shhh!" Gavril ordered, pulling me back down. "Stay low and follow me."

We obediently hunched over and followed Gavril's bent figure through the underbrush. I was so busy swatting branches out of my face that I didn't notice Gavril had stopped — until I ran into him.

Then Ron collided with me. It was like being hit by a tank.

"Timmy, give a guy some warning when you stop like that," Ron said, helping me up from the ground.

"Sorry, Ron. Gavril doesn't have brake lights."

Gavril shushed us. "Listen! Do you hear that?"

I listened.

Someone was calling for help!

"What do we do?" Kat asked.

"Follow me," Gavril said. "And be quiet!"

As we crept through the forest, the cries grew louder. Gavril paused at the edge of a clearing and carefully parted the bushes. We crowded around him, straining to see.

I couldn't believe my eyes.

Two soldiers were half-carrying, half-dragging a small, bearded man through the clearing. The little man was struggling against the ropes that tied his hands and feet and was yelling for help at the top of his lungs.

Please note: The following conversation was entirely spoken in whispers.

"Is that a dwarf?" I asked.

"We've got to help him," Kat said.

Gavril drew his sword. "I'll help him. You three stay here."

Ron grabbed his arm. "It'll be two against one out there. Let me come and even the odds."

"I can handle it. Just stay here and keep quiet. I don't want to have to worry about the three of you getting into trouble."

With a last warning look at us, Gavril stepped through the bushes into the clearing and approached the soldiers.

"Let the dwarf go," he said loudly.

"Wow, I was right!" I whispered to Ron and Kat. "He *is* a dwarf!"

I was quickly shushed.

The soldiers instantly obeyed Gavril's command, dropping the dwarf onto the grass. Then they drew their swords.

"Well, well, if it isn't our old friend, the ex-prince," one of them said. "The queen has been wanting to see you."

Gavril took another step forward. "I'll bet she has. Now move away from the dwarf, Kenley. And that goes for you, too, Tobbar," he said, indicating to the other soldier.

"Sure, Gavril," the man called Tobbar said, stepping over the dwarf. "I'd much rather take you back to the queen anyway and collect that nice, fat reward she's been offering."

Behind the bushes, Kat gasped. But out in the clearing, Gavril was keeping his cool.

"You're welcome to try," he said, lunging at Tobbar and starting the best sword fight I had ever seen.

No lie, Gavril was moving so quickly that his sword was practically a blur. It was like watching one of those old Errol Flynn movies my grandma likes. Only better.

"This is crazy," Kat whispered. "Gavril's going to get himself killed!"

Ron drew his sword. "No, he's not. I'm going out there."

Kat looked horrified. "Ron, no! You can't. You've never used a sword before!"

Ron paused and shrugged. "How hard can it be?" Then he parted the bushes and stepped through.

I called after him: "Ron, wait for me!"

Ignoring Kat's fiercely whispered protests, I plunged through the bushes after Ron. Our sudden entrance caught the attention of Kenley, who had been waiting his turn to take a stab at Gavril.

He walked over to us with a huge smile on his smug face.

"So, you little boys want to challenge Kenley, the queen's finest knight?" he asked, making little circles in the air with his sword in front of our faces.

My hands began to shake, and my palms got all sweaty, making it hard to hang onto my sword.

"Uh, challenge?" I said, my voice cracking a bit. "Yeah, sure. But I was thinking more of an arm wrestling match. Ron here is going to kick your butt."

Kenley laughed. "Oh, I'm going to enjoy cutting you two jesters into ribbons. And I'll start with you, little one!"

He pressed the point of his sword against my chest.

It hurt.

"Ron?" I squeaked, dropping my sword.

Ron raised his blade. "Leave him alone!"

His words were brave, but something about the tone of his voice told me he was wishing we had listened to Gavril and stayed behind the bushes.

Kenley spun toward Ron and thrust with his sword. Ron stepped quickly aside and swung wildly. Their blades met with a loud clank.

"Get him, Ron!" I yelled, scrambling a safe distance away.

Ron didn't even spare me a glance. But then again, he was a bit busy.

Kenley was lunging at him again and again, constantly encircling him and keeping him off balance. Ron blocked blow after blow, but it was hard work — even for someone as athletic as he was.

And eventually Ron began to get tired.

How did I know? Well, he was breathing hard and sweating a lot.

As for Kenley, the jerk looked as cool as the iceberg that sunk the Titanic.

And a bit bored.

Finally, Kenley gave a dramatic yawn and said, "As entertaining as this has been, it's time to end this little game."

With a quick twist of his wrist, he sent Ron's sword flying from his hand and leveled his blade at my brother's chest.

A surprised Ron stumbled backwards, tripped over a rock, and promptly landed flat on his back.

Kenley laughed and raised his sword high.

He was going to kill him! He was going to kill my brother!

"No!"

I made a flying leap, landed on Kenley's back, and latched onto his sword arm.

Brave of me? I thought so. But I was brushed off as easily as a mosquito and hit the ground with a thud.

In fact, my rescue attempt was over so quickly that Ron scarcely had time to move. Kenley turned back to him and raised his sword again.

I staggered to my feet with a hoarse yell.

But I knew there was no way I could stop him in time.

Ron was going to die.

Saved by a Girl

"**P**repare to meet your Maker," Kenley said, his arm muscles tensing to plunge his sword into my brother.

"No!" I yelled again. I tried to run toward them, but fear had frozen my legs. I felt like I was caught in quicksand.

"Please, no," I whispered, falling to my knees.

Then something dark whizzed over my head.

Kenley flinched and gave a cry of pain. As I watched in amazement, his arms dropped and his sword fell to the ground.

An arrow was sticking out of his shoulder.

An arrow?

Now where on earth did *that* come from?

With a grunt, Kenley pulled out the arrow and tossed it aside. Grasping his bleeding shoulder, he staggered across the clearing and disappeared into the woods without even a glance back.

I looked in shock at Ron, who looked back at me with an equally shocked expression on his face.

Then we wordlessly turned and looked across the clearing

Kat was standing under the trees, her face very pale. A bow was hanging loosely from her hand at her side.

My mouth dropped open. "Kat? You're the one who shot that guy?"

"Way to go, Kat!" Ron said. "I thought I was dead!"

He jumped to his feet and gave me a hand up. "That was a close one, wasn't it, Timmy? My whole life flashed before my eyes."

"Really?"

"Yeah. The part after I started dating was the most interesting—"

Ron broke off suddenly, raising his hands and ducking his head to protect himself. "Hey, hey! What are you doing?"

Kat had suddenly gone psycho and was hitting him with her bow!

Then she turned on me.

"Ow, Kat, stop it!" I said, trying to swat the bow away. "That thing hurts!"

"You two were almost killed!" Kat shouted, hitting us both once more. "Don't you *ever* scare me like that again!"

Then she flung down the bow and burst into tears.

Ron and I looked at each other.

"Do something," Ron whispered.

"No, you do something," I whispered back, giving him a little push.

Kat's head was down, her dark tangled hair hanging like a curtain and hiding her face. She was making those little noises people make when they're trying to stop crying.

Looking like he'd rather pet a tiger, Ron awkwardly began patting her shoulder. "Kat, are you okay?"

"No, I'm not (sniffle). If you haven't noticed (sniffle), I just shot a guy (sniffle)."

I noticed, and I was none too happy.

"Hey, Ron and I had that guy right where we wanted him. Why did you have to go and mess everything up?"

Kat lifted her head and glared at me. "I messed everything up? I shot a man to save your sorry butt, you ungrateful little jerk."

"No, you saved Ron's sorry butt. My butt was just fine, thank you."

Ron grasped me by the arm and pulled me aside. "What is wrong with you, Timmy? Why are you picking a fight with her? That guy would have killed us both if it wasn't for Kat, and you know it."

"Ron, we were just saved by our sister. A girl! Doesn't that bother you?"

Ron scratched his head. "Well yeah, it does when you put it that way."

"What's going on here?"

Ron and I spun around.

Gavril was coming toward us, his sword in his hand and fire in his eyes.

"Hey, Gavril," I said brightly. "Did you take care of that Tobbar guy?"

"He ran off when your sister shot Kenley. But what I want to know is why you're here in the clearing. I remember telling you to stay behind the bushes."

Ron looked at his feet. "Uh yeah, but you were out-numbered. We thought we could help you."

"Help me?" Gavril sheathed his sword with a look of exasperation. "If it wasn't for your sister, you and Tim would be dead right now!"

"I wish people would stop saying that," I said. "It was just a lucky shot."

"It was not!" Kat said.

"Was too!"

"Enough!" Gavril shouted.

Kat and I cut our argument short and looked at him. Ron was still busy studying his shoes.

Gavril took a deep breath and let it out. "Look, we have a hard and dangerous road ahead of us. I need to know I can count on you. When I tell you boys to do something, you need to do it. Do you understand?"

Ron nodded wordlessly.

Gavril locked eyes with me. "Tim?"

I looked away, feeling about two inches tall. "Yeah, I understand."

"Gavril, if you're done giving those young people a tongue-lashing, I could use a hand over here!"

I smacked my palm to my forehead. "The dwarf! We forgot all about him!"

"Little person," Kat said.

Whatever. As long as he took Gavril's attention away from me, I didn't care what he was called.

Gavril pushed past us and walked over to where the dwarf (sorry, "little person") had been dumped by the soldiers on the ground.

"I'm so sorry, Beriman," Gavril said, stooping down to his level. "We've been neglecting you."

Beriman looked up at him, his red tasseled cap covering one eye. "Just cut me loose. These ropes are killing me."

Gavril sliced through the ropes with his dagger, and the dwarf leapt to his feet. He quickly straightened his cap, brushed bits of leaves and grass off his light blue tunic, and fluffed his long, bushy beard.

"Are you hurt?" Gavril asked.

"No, my good man. But I am tremendously in your debt. It's fortunate you came along when you did. Is the king well?"

"He is fine."

"I'm glad to hear it."

But Gavril was apparently not in the mood for small talk. He got right down to business.

"Beriman, my father and I were ambushed upon our return from the north country. What happened in Tryton while we were gone? I must know."

A shadow crossed Beriman's face. "During your absence, the queen grew in power. All who stood against her, like the dwarves, were either thrown into her dungeon or forced to work in her mines. It's from one of the mines that I escaped, only to be recaptured by those two ruffians."

"How awful!" Kat said.

Beriman peered around Gavril to look at us. "And who are these youngsters?"

Gavril gave a little sigh. "Beriman, I'd like to present to you Ron Hunter and his siblings Kat and Tim. They *claim* to have come through the mirror from another world."

Beriman stroked his beard thoughtfully. "Not the mirror in Fenimore Castle?"

"The very same."

"How odd," Beriman said. "This is the second time in a matter of months that someone has come through that mirror."

"Someone else has come through?" Kat asked. "Who?"

"A couple of brothers named Jacob and Wilhelm

Grimm."

"The Brothers Grimm?" Kat asked. "The guys who wrote the fairy tales?"

I shrugged. "Makes sense. Uncle Edgar said the mirror once belonged to them."

"What fairy tales?" Ron asked.

"You know," Kat said. "*Cinderella, Snow White and the Seven Dwarves,* and a bunch of others."

"I thought Walt Disney wrote those," Ron said.

Kat rolled her eyes and was about to respond when Gavril held up his hand.

"We don't have time for this right now," he said. "We have a lot of ground to cover before nightfall."

"Where are you headed in such a hurry?" Beriman asked.

"We're going to the castle in Tryton to steal the queen's mirror," I said.

Beriman's mouth dropped open. "Gavril, with all due respect, are you out of your mind? You should be storming the castle with a troop of your best soldiers — not with these children."

Gavril nodded in agreement. "That's exactly what I told the king. But he seems to think they're the ones from the prophecy."

"Really?" Beriman's fuzzy eyebrows shot up, and he looked at us like he was seeing us for the first time. "Too bad they don't know one end of the sword from the other."

"Hey, it was our first battle," I said. "Give us a break."

"Well, it looks like you could use some help," Beriman said. "I only wish I still had my pickaxe. Those soldiers took it from me and flung it into the bushes somewhere."

"You may use Kenley's sword, if you'd like," Gavril said, picking it up off the ground, "but I'm afraid it will be too long for you."

Beriman took the weapon and deftly tried a few strikes in the air. "It will do."

Sticking the sword in his belt — and ignoring the fact that its tip was dragging on the ground — Beriman looked up and said: "Shall we go?"

Gavril clapped a hand on Beriman's shoulder. "I'm very glad you are with us, my friend. You don't know what a relief it is to have someone else in our group that can handle a sword."

Yep, it was official. Gavril thought we were losers.

Shocker.

Sword Fighting for Dummies

Acting like he didn't just insult us, Gavril plunged onto a little path that snaked its way through the woods, expecting us to follow like a herd of well-trained mountain goats.

Which, of course, we did.

But I trailed along at the end of the line, feeling about as low as a worm.

Gavril was right. I had messed up my first sword fight.

Big time.

I couldn't even hang onto my sword for more than two seconds!

I was just a loser.

The worst part was that I had to be saved by my sister. I'll never live it down. Ever. If my friends in school ever found out...

"Something's not right," Kat said, interrupting my thoughts.

Gavril stopped and looked back. "What is it? Are we being followed?"

"No. I was just thinking about the Brothers Grimm."

"Oh, that." Gavril pushed ahead on the trail. I would almost bet he was rolling his eyes and muttering to himself up there.

"When exactly were they here?" Kat asked.

Beriman shrugged. "A few months ago."

"But that doesn't make sense. Jacob and Wilhelm Grimm lived in the 1800s. That was over two hundred years ago."

"Maybe time passes differently here than in your world," Beriman said.

Kat frowned. "Maybe."

"Are they still here, Beriman?" I asked.

"Who?"

"The Grimm brothers. It would be cool to meet them."

"No, they didn't stay long."

Bummer.

"So, what brave thing did they do to get home through the mirror?"

"Good question, Tim." Beriman thought for a moment. "I think they rescued a baby from a runaway horse."

Great. They stole our idea.

Our conversation dwindled away after that because we needed our breath for the hike.

Remember how I said earlier that walking through the woods was almost pleasant?

I take it all back.

We had reached what Gavril called "the foothills," and the trail was growing steeper.

Soon I was huffing and puffing my way up the hills like one of those old steam engine trains. I would have been embarrassed, but everyone else was struggling, too.

Yes, even Ron. A little.

The only real exception was Gavril. You'd think he was taking a leisurely stroll through a meadow or something. At one point, he was even whistling.

I can't tell you how annoying that was.

It was nearly dark — and I was nearly dropping from exhaustion — when Gavril finally halted in the middle of a fairly level clearing and announced it was time to stop for the night.

Everyone (except Gavril) flopped down on the ground, but our mighty leader wasn't about to let us stay there for long.

"On your feet, people," he said, clapping his hands. "We need to set up camp."

Kat stirred first. "I'll fetch some water."

Grabbing the empty water skins, she walked stiffly over to a nearby creek.

Beriman stood up next and smacked Ron on the shoulder. "Come on, Ron Hunter. Let's go gather some wood for the fire."

I sat up and watched them disappear into the woods. That left me alone with Gavril.

Great.

Gavril dropped down beside me. "You're being unusually quiet, Tim."

I shrugged.

"What's wrong?"

"Nothing."

"Did Kenley hurt you?"

"No."

Except for my pride, of course. But I wasn't about to tell *him* that.

"That's good. Things could have turned out

much worse. It's very fortunate your sister knows how to handle a bow."

That did it.

"Why does everyone keep saying that? She got lucky, okay?"

Gavril shook his head. "I saw her make the shot. She knows what she's doing."

I gave a sigh. "She belongs to an archery club at school. Besides, she's perfect at everything she does. So is Ron — when it comes to sports."

Academic stuff, not so much.

"What about you?"

"I'm terrible at everything."

I couldn't believe I said that out loud — and to Gavril, of all people. But it was true. I really was a loser.

Gavril was quiet for a moment. "Don't be so hard on yourself," he finally said. "You just don't know how to use a sword."

No kidding.

Nudging me with his shoulder, Gavril said softly: "I might be able to help you with that."

I stared at him. "What are you talking about?"

"I can teach you how to fight."

My mouth dropped open. "Are you serious?"

Gavril grinned. "I'm always serious."

True.

Ron dumped a load of firewood next to us. "Hey Gavril, did I just hear you promise to teach Timmy to sword fight?"

"Yes, he needs a bit of help."

"I do, too. Can I get in on that?"

"Sure. I can teach you two the basics, which will be enough to keep you from getting killed." He cleared his throat. "Maybe."

Beriman gave a little chuckle and started stacking the firewood. "You've got your work cut out for you, Gavril, so you'd better get started right away. I'll get the fire going."

"Thank you, Beriman. Ron and Tim, go get your swords."

I couldn't help but let out a happy squeal as I ran for my sword. I sounded like a little girl, but I didn't care.

Kat chose that moment to return with the full water skins. "What's going on?"

I grinned at her. I couldn't wipe the smile off my face if I tried. "Gavril is teaching me to sword fight!"

"What?" Kat threw the water skins to the ground and marched over to Gavril. "Are you insane? Timmy can't use a sword. He's just a kid! He'll put his eye out — or be killed!"

"That's exactly why he needs some training," Gavril said. "I'm trying to keep that from happening."

Kat shook her head. "But you don't know Timmy like I do. He's a klutz!"

"I am not!"

Gavril shrugged. "All the more reason to teach him how to fight."

Kat's arms crossed over her chest. "I don't like it."

"The boy needs this," Gavril said. "Just trust me."

Kat hesitated. She was as likely to trust Gavril as I was to get my belly button pierced. I made one last desperate plea.

"Please, Kat. You don't want me to be a sitting

duck if we're attacked by soldiers or galrogs, do you? I need to be able to defend myself."

Kat stared at me, biting her lip.

"I promise to be careful," I added in the most sincere tone I could muster. I meant it, too. Kind of.

Kat sighed. "Fine. But if you get yourself killed, Timmy, your blood is on your hands."

I shrugged. I could live with that.

Sneak Attack

Fast-forward a couple of hours.

There I was, lying under the night sky and trying to fall asleep, while re-living every humiliating moment of my first sword-fighting lesson.

I couldn't help but wonder why I was so eager for a lesson with Gavril in the first place. All I did was drop my sword a bazillion times. Gavril looked totally frustrated with me.

Oh, and if you're wondering, Ron did great. Mr. "Sports Star" was practically a pro by the end of the lesson.

Surprised?

Me neither.

Feeling sorry for myself, I rolled over on my side, closed my eyes, and hoped sleep would come.

That was when I heard the rustling sound.

Don't laugh. I know perfectly well that forests are full of rustling sounds. Especially at night. But this noise was different. It was somehow louder — and closer.

And scarier.

I sat up and looked around.

The rustling noise sounded again, but I couldn't see anything. The fire was already burning low, making the clearing dark and full of shadows.

Ron had let it go down again. Great. If something was about to jump out of the woods and attack me, I wanted to at least see what it was. I needed to build up the fire to get more light — and fast.

I got quietly to my feet and worked my way over to the pile of branches Ron and Beriman had gathered earlier. I took special care not to step on anyone — especially Kat. She would totally kill me.

I stooped over, lifted a branch from the pile, and froze, my heart beating in my throat.

Eyes.

I saw freakish yellow eyes at the edge of the clearing.

And they were looking right at me!

Startled, I gave a little yell.

The eyes disappeared in a blink.

A bundle on the ground stirred.

"Timmy, what is wrong with you?" Kat said. "Are you trying to wake us all up?"

"Eyes!" I whispered. "I saw yellow eyes in the bushes over there!"

Gavril was on his feet immediately with his sword drawn. Yeah, I was terrified, but I still couldn't help but be impressed with how fast he moved.

"Galrog," Gavril said, his voice grim.

I stared at him. "Not those things that tear you to pieces."

"I'm afraid so."

"What do we do?" Kat asked. She sounded scared.

"Get the others up and put more wood on the fire."

"But Gavril," I said. "I thought you said fire doesn't bother galrogs."

"It doesn't. But it'll give us some light to fight by."

Fight? Was he kidding?

Fighting galrogs was near the bottom of my to-do list, landing somewhere between swimming with piranha and wrestling a grizzly bear. But I hurried to do what Gavril said anyway — and discovered that the word "galrog" wakes up Ron better than any air horn ever did.

Within mere moments, the fire was burning brighter, and we were standing close to it, weapons in hand and eyes peering into the darkness that hovered at the edge of the clearing.

Gavril stood a short distance away, his sword ready.

A twig snapped.

With shaking hands, Kat strung her bow and quickly fitted an arrow to the string.

I gripped my sword so hard my hand hurt.

Suddenly, there was a snarl, and a large creature leapt from the shadows into the clearing.

And I got my first good look at a galrog.

It wasn't pretty.

Picture a creature that has the strong, square jaw of a pit bull. Add the lean, muscular body of a panther. Triple the size, and throw in some unusually long, sharp teeth.

And that's basically what I saw.

Horrible, right?

Well, to make matters even worse, it had friends.

We barely had a chance to react to that first galrog before *more* creatures jumped out on all sides of the clearing. They were lightning-fast, and their eyes glowed like coals from the fire.

I couldn't move. I just stood there clutching my useless sword and praying that none of those things came near me.

Gavril let out a roar, which alarmed me almost as much as the galrogs, and charged with his sword.

Ron and Beriman followed him, with Ron looking fierce and confidant for someone who just had his first sword-fighting lesson a few hours earlier.

Even Kat got into the fray, letting fly one arrow after another.

All I could do was helplessly watch the battle unfold before me. It was like being caught in the middle of the worst nightmare ever.

In the flickering light of the fire, shadows were leaping, swords were swinging, and arrows were flying. I could hear the cries of my companions, the growls of the galrogs, and the impact of weapons against flesh.

It was awful.

I felt like being sick.

I knew I should get out there and help them, but there was NO WAY I was going to fight one of those things. I decided to stick close to the fire and hope the bright flames would keep the galrogs away.

Talk about wishful thinking.

A low growl sounded close by, and I whirled around to find myself facing the largest, fiercest animal I had ever seen.

Mindless of the fire, it crept forward, its unblinking yellow eyes fixed on me.

My heart shot up into my throat, and my legs

turned to rubber. I struggled to hold onto my trembling sword.

"Nice doggy."

The creature crouched, its tail twitching and the muscles tensing in its massive hind legs.

Saliva dripped from its fangs.

Yes, it had FANGS!

I didn't have to be an expert at reading galrog body language to know I was about two seconds away from becoming the creature's late night snack.

"Somebody, help!" I squeaked.

"Timmy!" Kat screamed. She sounded terrified, and she should be. Her baby brother was about to be eaten by a galrog.

An arrow flew by me and narrowly missed the creature.

"Watch it, Kat! You almost got *me!*"

The galrog curled its lips and snarled briefly in Kat's direction before turning those yellow eyes back on me. Fear had me frozen again, and everything seemed to shift into slow motion.

The galrog bunched up its muscles and sprang into the air.

"No!" Kat's scream sounded as if it came from a distance.

I raised my sword in front of me and shielded my face with my other arm.

There was a moment of intense confusion, filled with flashing teeth and sharp claws, and then a crushing weight knocked me to the ground.

Crying out, I struggled, pushing with all my might against the coarse fur.

Suddenly, the weight rolled off of me, and I scrambled to my feet, breathing hard. I looked

around wildly, wondering what became of the galrog
— and my sword.

Yep, I had lost my sword. Again.

"Nice work, Tim." Gavril clapped a hand on my
shoulder and gave me a weary smile. "That was a big
one."

My mouth dropped open, and I stared at him. A
compliment from Gavril? Maybe I was hallucinating.

Or maybe I had died.

"A big one? What are you talking about?"

Gavril gestured toward the ground, and I was
surprised to see a large, dark shape lying there with a
sword sticking out of its side.

The galrog... and my sword...

So that's where they went to!

"Is it dead?" (The galrog, not the sword.)

Gavril drew out the sword and handed it to me.
"Very. We got most of them. Only a couple got
away."

But I had stopped listening. I had killed a galrog!
Me! Tim Hunter: Galrog Slayer!

Kat rushed up to us. "Tim, are you alright?"

Did you hear that? Tim! She called me Tim! I felt
myself grow twelve inches taller.

"Yeah, of course. I had that galrog right where I
wanted him the whole time."

"Sure you did," Kat said, but she looked
relieved.

Ron and Beriman came up, and I swear my big
bro had a bit of swagger in his step.

"Wow," he said, "That was unbelievable. If I
didn't know any better, I'd think those galrogs were
organized or something."

"They probably were," Gavril said. "Rumor has

it that the queen captured some galrogs and trained them to do her bidding."

"Are you saying the queen *sent* these galrogs to attack us?" I asked.

Gavril shrugged. "It's possible."

"Then, we just killed off some of her pets. I don't think she's going to like us very much."

"Wait a minute," Kat said. "If the queen sent these horrible creatures after us, then she knows we're coming."

Ron scoffed. "That's dumb. How could she know?"

"Maybe those soldiers we fought told her," I said.

"Or," Gavril said. "She's seen us in the mirror."

I frowned. "But I thought the king said that was impossible."

"Yeah," Kat said. "He practically promised us that she wouldn't know to ask the mirror about us."

Gavril sighed. "I know. But my father tends to be overly optimistic.

"So she knows we're coming?" Kat was practically shouting now.

"I don't know—"

But Kat wasn't listening. "Then she'll be waiting for us. She'll kill us! We need to turn back now!"

"Kat, just stop it!" Gavril said. "We can't know any of that for certain. I was just saying that it's a possibility she saw us in the mirror. A possibility."

"So maybe the galrogs found us by accident?" Ron asked.

"Maybe."

"But maybe they didn't," Kat said.

Gavril sighed. "There's no way we can know for

sure. The truth is that we could be walking into a trap."

"Then it's too dangerous," Kat said. "We must turn back."

"But what will happen if we do?" Gavril asked. "Do you really think the queen will be satisfied with my father's little kingdom? She wants more power and more land. Many lives are at stake. That's why we need to take the risk and try to stop her."

Gavril paused and looked at each one of us. "We'll take a vote. If you think we should continue with our mission, raise your hand."

Beriman's hand popped up. Then Ron's. And mine quickly followed.

I'm Tim the Galrog Slayer. What have I got to be afraid of?

Kat gave a little sigh. "Fine. We'll go on. But how are we supposed to get into the castle if the queen is expecting us?"

Gavril shrugged. "We'll think of something."

In other words, Gavril didn't have a plan.

Great.

False Alarms

We broke camp in a hurry.

Yeah, I know it was still the middle of the night. Normally, I would *not* be okay with that. I'm a growing boy, and I need my sleep.

But none of us felt like spending the rest of the night in the clearing with a bunch of dead galrogs. So we cleaned our weapons (Gavril insisted on that), packed up our things, and hit the trail.

I immediately had regrets. The steep trail would have been tough if we were starting out on it fresh in the morning. But climbing a mountain in the dark when you've had almost no sleep — and had just been fighting for your life — well, that kind of sucks big time.

I stumbled up the mountain half-asleep, grabbing onto branches, rocks, and even Kat to help me keep moving forward.

Well, I actually only grabbed onto Kat *once*. To be honest, it didn't go over well.

She sure can be touchy when she doesn't get enough sleep.

Actually, walking uphill in the dark and getting smacked in the face by unseen branches didn't do much to improve any of our moods. So when I noticed the sky growing brighter, I couldn't help but be relieved.

Morning was coming! I would have broken out into a happy dance right there on the mountainside, but I was too tired.

Unfortunately, my relief didn't last long. As the sun began to rise, the fog moved in. A lot of it. All around us, wisps of mist messed with our vision and made the forest seem even creepier than it was.

Gavril finally stopped to get his bearings and give us a breather. (He didn't need one himself, of course.)

"We've done well, everyone. We're almost at the top."

"Yay!" I said rather weakly from where I was sprawled out on the ground.

"How can you tell in all this fog?" Kat asked.

Gavril turned his steely gaze on her. "I know this trail like the back of my hand. We're getting close to the pass."

"The pass is a great spot for an ambush if you ask me," Beriman said.

"What?" I sat up so fast my head spun. "We're going to be ambushed?"

Gavril sighed. "Tim."

"But we haven't even had breakfast yet!"

"Tim, take it easy."

"But, Gavril, there could be like twenty soldiers waiting for us at the pass. You heard Beriman."

"Tim."

"And in this fog, we wouldn't see them until it's too late. And then we'd be dead."

Beriman was laughing. "Tim, I was only thinking out loud. Just because the pass would be a good place for an ambush doesn't necessarily mean anyone is waiting for us there."

"Yeah, the queen's soldiers are probably all still in bed, which is where I'd like to be," Ron said with a big yawn.

"Let's just keep moving," Gavril said. "And stay alert through the pass, which is what you should be doing anyway. We're not on a walking holiday, you know."

No kidding.

Fortunately, we didn't have to go much farther before the ground started to level off, and the going got a bit easier.

The fog was beginning to break up a little, too. Looking up, I could just make out the dark, towering shapes of Mount Kern on the left and Mount Omer on the right. Or was it the other way around? Gavril had pointed out the mountains earlier, but I was terrible at geography.

Either way, the pass must be close.

Suddenly, there was a loud crash. A large, dark shape leapt onto the trail in front of us.

Totally taken by surprise, Kat screamed, I squeaked, and Ron yelled: "It's the ambush!"

One or two of us drew our swords.

Okay, to be more accurate (and honest), Gavril and Beriman drew their swords. I momentarily forgot I had one.

Gavril laughed as he watched the creature nimbly bound away. "It's just a deer! How fortunate for you, since you three weren't prepared to defend yourselves."

"I knew it was a deer the whole time," I said.

"Sure you did."

"Can we just keep going?" Ron said, his face flushed.

I could tell he was embarrassed about the deer incident. He pushed past Gavril with his head down and walked on ahead. But when he reached the top of the slope, he stopped short on the trail and said: "Wow!"

"Wow what?" I asked. I trotted ahead and slipped past him. Then I stopped, too. "Cool!"

We had finally reached the top of the pass, and the valley was spread out before us. The mist had broken up enough to give us quite a view.

Rolling green fields were dotted with spots of white fluff that could only be sheep, and quaint little farms were scattered here and there. Right in the center was a cluster of buildings that looked very much like the medieval villages I had seen in movies.

Kat squeezed by me to get a look. "Check out that castle!"

How could I miss it? Standing tall at the edge of the village was the most beautiful castle I had ever seen.

Its white walls and turrets gleamed gold in the morning sun. It was more magnificent than anything Walt Disney ever dreamed up. I couldn't take my eyes off of it.

"Is that Tryton?" Ron asked.

"Yes, it is," Gavril said quietly.

"That castle is where the queen lives," Beriman said, pointing rather unnecessarily.

Like I said, the castle was hard to miss.

"I thought it would be dark and scary, but it's not," Kat said. "It's really beautiful. I can't wait to see it up close."

"What are you going to do, Kat?" I asked. "Have the queen give you a tour?"

"Of course not! Don't be stupid."

"*You're* the one acting stupid."

"If you ask me, you're *both* acting stupid," Ron said.

"No one asked you," said Kat.

Beriman looked at Gavril. "Are they always like this?"

Gavril sighed. "Yes."

Beriman shook his head and made a tsk-tsk noise.

Gavril patted his shoulder. "Let's keep moving."

As he started down the trail with Beriman, we abandoned our mini-argument and scrambled after him. But we didn't get far before my stomach started to growl.

"I'm hungry."

Gavril paused, looking thoughtful. "I guess we could take a little break. I know just the place."

He broke off the trail into the underbrush and called over his shoulder, "Follow me!"

"Hey, where are you taking us?" I asked.

"This had better be good," Kat said, battling her way past a thorny bush.

Suddenly, we came upon a huge boulder. It was perfectly flat on top — like someone had stuck a big stone platform right in the middle of the forest.

We scrambled up onto it (after giving Beriman a boost) and settled down to eat breakfast. The stone was already warm from the morning sun and the view of the valley was really something.

"This is great," Kat said between bites of deer jerky.

I decided she was talking about the view, not the food. The jerky was getting a bit old — in more ways than one.

Gavril was staring out into the valley.

"We need to consider the route we should take to the castle," he said, pointing. "Do you see those hills that branch off of Mount Kern and hug the west side of the valley? If we go that way, we would be able to stay under the cover of the forest longer and avoid going through the village."

"But there are mines in those hills," Beriman said, "so there's a good chance soldiers will be in the area. We might be spotted."

"I admit there's a risk, Beriman, but it's still better than marching through the center of the village."

"Go west, young man," I said. "That's what I always say."

"Why do you always say that?" Beriman asked.

I shrugged with a laugh. "I don't know. I just heard it somewhere."

"Then west it is." Gavril leapt off the rock with the agility of an acrobat and looked up at us from below.

"Come on. Let's get going. The way is longer than you'd think, and I'd like to get there before nightfall."

I shoved the last bit of my deer jerky into my mouth and followed the others down off the rock. And no, I did not imitate Gavril and leap off from the top. Knowing my luck, I would break an ankle or something. And I needed two good ankles to get down that mountain.

Not only did we have to fight our way through the underbrush to get back to the trail, but the path itself was narrow and windy. I could only assume it was created by some mountain goats with a lousy sense of direction.

We traveled back and forth and up and down (mostly down) on that twisty-turny trail for hours. I was yawning and wishing for a nap when Gavril started motioning to us to be quiet.

The mine entrance was up ahead. Through the screen of leaves, I could just make out a gaping hole in the mountainside guarded by two soldiers.

With multiple hand motions, Gavril directed us off the path and led us through the undergrowth around the mine. With our heads tucked down, we were creeping past the opening as quietly as a summer breeze — until a dry twig snapped under my foot with a loud crack.

I froze. The others froze. Kat shot me a look that accused me of being an idiot. (Trust me. I've seen that look before.)

But we needn't have worried. The soldiers were so deep in conversation about a village girl named Mandie — who was a "comely lass," whatever that means — that we could have rode by on unicycles while blowing horns, and they wouldn't have noticed us anyway.

We were back on the trail and continuing our hike downhill with the soldiers being none the wiser.

It wasn't until about mid-afternoon that the scenery began to change. The ground became more level, the trees and underbrush had thinned out nicely, and the path was wider and smoother.

We started making better time, which should

have made Gavril happy. But no. He looked more anxious than a hamster in a room full of clumsy elephants.

"This could be the most dangerous part of our journey," he said, glancing around. "There aren't enough trees to hide us here. Anyone coming along the road could easily see us."

Ron looked surprised. "There's a road?"

"Yes, it's a stone's throw that way," Gavril said, pointing. "It leads back up to the mines, and it's well-traveled, I'm afraid."

Kat stiffened. "Like now! I think I hear someone coming!"

"Kat, stop kidding around," Ron said.

"I'm not!"

Gavril threw up his hand. "Silence!"

I strained my ears. As much as I hated to admit it, Kat was right. I could definitely hear the pounding of hooves in the distance.

But not only that, I could see them.

A squad of horsemen was thundering up the road in a cloud of dust.

There was no way they could miss us.

The Welcoming Committee

"**F**ollow me!"

Gavril dashed over to where three trees with white, peeling bark grew closely together. We scrambled after him and jostled for a position behind them.

Of course, the trees couldn't provide enough cover for all of us. So some of us (mainly me) had to settle for lying down behind some sorry-looking bushes next to them.

But I'm proud to say we handled this stressful moment with our usual calmness and self-control.

"Timmy, get your head down," Kat whispered. "They'll see you!"

"I'm trying, but Ron's big, fat foot is in my way."

"How is my foot in your way?"

"It's right where I need to put my face!"

"My foot is not in your way."

"Just move your foot, Ron!" Gavril said.

Ron did. So my head was properly lowered when the horsemen streamed by in a flurry of flying manes and hooves.

But you know what? The men kept their faces set forward. They never even glanced our way once.

All that fuss for nothing.

Gavril stepped out from behind the trees and gave me a hand up. "All's clear. Let's keep moving."

And off we went across the "plain" - as Gavril called it - falling into line behind him like ducklings behind their mama.

Yeah, he had us well-trained.

We had to hide behind trees and bushes whenever someone appeared on the road. But, otherwise, that portion of our journey was just as boring as the mountainside.

Judging by the grumbling of my stomach, it was almost suppertime when I finally saw a tall wall in the distance. Just beyond it — with stone towers that stretched up toward the sky — stood a massive white building that looked like it belonged in a book of fairy tales.

The castle.

My heart started to beat a little faster. I was beginning to see why Gavril had his doubts about the success of our mission. How were we supposed to get over that huge wall? I was pretty sure we didn't have any climbing gear with us.

"Keep an eye open for soldiers," Gavril said. "The queen has patrols around the castle."

Great. High walls *and* soldiers. That settled it. We had as much chance of getting into that castle as Ron did of making straight A's.

I sighed to myself. If we were going to have an epic fail — and probably die in the process — I just wanted to get it over with. But for some strange reason, Gavril *slowed* down our pace.

We would scuttle behind a bush and wait, wait, wait. Then, we'd scurry ahead a few feet to the nearest clump of trees and wait, wait, wait. And then we were off to another bush about five feet away for another round of — you guessed it — *waiting*.

I swear I saw a snail making better time than we were.

After what seemed like an eternity, we finally made it to a couple of rhododendron bushes about fifty yards from the outer wall. But just as we were about to move forward, Gavril thrust out his hand.

"Soldiers! Stay down!"

More waiting.

I hunkered lower in the grass and peered under the lowest branches of the bush. "Where? I don't see them."

"Timmy, shut up," Kat hissed.

"You shut up."

"You *both* shut up," Gavril whispered fiercely. "And look."

I looked. A squad of soldiers was rounding the corner of the wall. I stayed as still as possible and watched them as they marched.

They looked bored, but at least they were moving along quickly. It took only a minute or so for them to disappear around the far corner and presumably continue their endless trek around the castle.

The moment the soldiers' footsteps faded away, Gavril leapt to his feet. "Follow me, and keep quiet."

As we ran up to the wall, I noticed something surprising.

There was no moat.

What self-respecting castle didn't have a moat?

I went up to Gavril, who was busy searching for something behind a curtain of vines that covered one section of the wall.

"Why is there no moat?" I whispered.

Gavril paused and gave me a look that clearly said I was bothering him. But he sighed and answered back (in a whisper, of course).

"When my father built this castle, the land was at peace. He didn't need to include a moat. Besides," he added, turning his attention back to the vines, "moats attract mosquitoes."

Oh.

"Gavril, what are you looking for behind those vines?" Ron whispered.

"Ivy," Kat whispered.

"What?"

"The vines. They're ivy."

Ron rolled his eyes, clearing showing how little he cared about that specific piece of information.

Gavril ignored them both. Pushing apart another clump of vines — excuse me, *ivy* — he stopped. "There it is."

He had uncovered an old door set into the wall. Its wood had faded to a grayish color which made it almost invisible against the stones.

With a warning glance at us to keep quiet, Gavril lifted the heavy iron latch and pushed. The door opened with a screech of rusty hinges, making me jump.

"Way to go, Gavril," I whispered. "Now the whole world knows we're here."

Gavril shushed me with another look and motioned for us to follow him through the doorway. I tried to act casual about it, but my heart was breakdancing on my ribs.

This was enemy territory, remember?

What if the queen was waiting for us? What if the grounds of the castle were guarded by patrolling herds of galrogs? What if a squad of soldiers was waiting just inside?

But all of my worries fled away as I entered the wildest, most beautiful garden I had ever seen.

Now, don't go thinking I'm one of those guys who love flowers. I'm not. I can't tell a pansy from a petunia. But I can recognize a rose — and that place was full of them.

They were blooming in bushes, climbing up walls, and dangling from trellises in an astounding variety of colors and shapes.

My mom, who loves to garden, would go nuts to see them.

I could tell Kat liked them, too, although she was more into the decorations in the garden. As we followed Gavril down a little stone path, she oohed and aahed whenever she spotted a stone bench or a statue of a girl dancing.

And when Kat saw the large fountain topped with a stained and ugly stone cherub, she almost lost her mind.

Don't ask me why. It was just a stupid fountain. And it wasn't even working!

As for Gavril, he barely spared the garden a glance. He went straight to another ivy-covered wall and began searching again.

"Looking for another door?" I whispered.

"Yes, the back way into the castle," Gavril whispered back. "I'm hoping the queen has forgotten about it."

His knuckles hit what sounded like wood and his face lit up. "And here it is."

Sweeping aside a curtain of ivy, Gavril revealed another ancient-looking door. I just hoped it didn't squeak as badly as the last one. My nerves couldn't take it.

I held my breath as Gavril lifted the latch and pulled.

Nothing.

Not a screech. Not even a squeak. The door slid open without a peep. And we all crowded around to take a look.

A long stone passageway stretched out before us — lit by torches that were hung from brackets on the walls.

"Why are the lights on?" I whispered.

"The queen requires the corridors to be lit at all times," Gavril whispered back, stepping inside and taking a cautious look around. "If a servant lets a torch go out, he is severely punished."

"Great. What does she do if she catches trespassers?"

Gavril gave me a glance. "You don't want to know."

Beriman sighed and pushed past me into the passageway. "Let's get this over with."

I couldn't agree with him more. But that didn't help me feel any braver as we started down the corridor. Despite the torches, it seemed dark and creepy. And our footsteps echoed off the stone floor — no matter how softly we tried to walk.

We crept forward cautiously and soon approached a set of heavy, wooden doors, one on each side of the corridor.

Gavril paused and gestured for us to stop. I could almost see his ears straining as he listened for the slightest sound of movement behind those doors. There was complete silence. You could have heard a pin drop.

Apparently satisfied that the doors were safe to pass, Gavril motioned us onward.

But I swear I saw one of those doors move. Just a little.

Now, I probably should had said something to Gavril then and there, but I didn't. Maybe the door was stirred by a breeze coming in through a window. I didn't want to risk looking like an idiot.

But that didn't mean I couldn't check it out for myself.

A quick glance told me the others had continued walking down the corridor and were paying no attention to me at all.

Perfect.

I turned my attention back to the door and cautiously nudged at it with the toe of my sneaker.

It swung open about an inch.

I looked up and gave a gasp.

An eye! It was staring at me through the gap!

And, unless I was mistaken, it belonged to a soldier!

Without thinking, I pulled the door shut. The handle began to jerk under my hand, and I held onto it with all my strength.

Of course, I'm a 12-year-old toothpick, so that's not saying much.

Gavril flew back down the corridor toward me. "Tim, what do you think you're doing?"

"Soldier! In the room! Saw me!"

Understanding flashed across Gavril's face. "Come on."

He grabbed my arm and pulled me down the hallway toward the others.

"What's going on?" Ron asked.

Gavril gave him a push. "Get moving! Now!"

"Why? What's happening?"

Kat screamed and pointed down the passageway. Soldiers were pouring out through the door I had opened and were filling the corridor. Their swords were drawn, and they were coming right at us.

"Run!" Gavril shouted, pushing me ahead of him and drawing his sword.

We ran all right. But we only made it about five feet before the other end of the passageway filled with another group of well-armed soldiers.

Great. We were surrounded.

"Draw your weapons," Gavril cried, "and stand back to back." He took a deep breath. "And do not panic."

Too late. I was already panicking. But I obeyed the rest of Gavril's instructions and pulled out my sword.

Don't be too impressed. I was shaking so badly that it was next to useless.

I watched as Ron and Beriman drew their swords from their sheaths, and Kat strung her bow. It made me feel a little better to see that Kat's hands were shaking, too.

"Gavril, this isn't going to work," Beriman said. "I don't know if you've noticed or not, but we're considerably out-numbered!"

"Would you rather we surrender without a fight?" Gavril asked, his eyes on the advancing soldiers.

"No!" Beriman said, gripping his sword even tighter. "Dwarves never surrender!"

"Can we vote on this?" I asked.

Ron shook his head. "We are so dead."

The Dungeon

Thankfully, Ron's prediction was wrong. Well, it was for the moment, anyway. The soldiers abruptly stopped about six feet from us and just stared.

And stared.

I felt myself start to sweat.

"What are they doing?" I whispered to Gavril, wishing they'd do something. Anything! (Well, almost anything.) The suspense was killing me.

Before Gavril could answer me, a shout sounded from farther up the corridor: "Make way for Queen Morissa!"

In one cool, synchronized movement, the soldiers split into two groups, creating a gap for a woman to walk through.

"Wow," Ron whispered.

Wow was right. One look at the queen, and I forgot all about the soldiers.

Why? Well, imagine taking the most gorgeous supermodel and combining her with the most beautiful actress and adding long, fiery red hair.

Yeah, the queen looked *that* good. Poor Ron was almost hyperventilating.

"Hello, Gavril," the queen said. "I was expecting you, my son."

"*Son*?" I stared at Gavril. "You're her son?"

Gavril kept his eyes fixed on the queen. "No, I'm

not. She married my father after my mother died. That's all."

"*That's all?*" Kat said, looking mad enough to chew up an entire box of nails and spit them at him. "Your father was married to *this woman,* and you're just mentioning it *now?*"

"What do you mean 'this woman?'" the queen asked Kat.

"Well, everyone knows you're evil."

"Not helping, Kat," Ron muttered.

The queen laughed. "So that's what the king has told you, is it? Well, let me tell you something, young lady. No one gets ahead in this life by being nice and accommodating. If you want something, you need to take it."

"You already had my father's kingdom," Gavril said. "You were his wife."

"Yes, but it's so small. I wanted to, uh, *expand* into other lands. But your father lacked ambition. That's why he and his rag-tag group of followers had to go."

Gavril's normally cool eyes flared with anger. "So you waited for us to return from our visit to my sister's kingdom and ambushed us."

The queen shrugged. "How else could I take over his kingdom? Soon, I will be the most powerful queen in all the world. And no one will be able to stop me."

"Especially not you and those three children," she added with an elegant sniff. "I don't care what some old prophecy says."

Gavril's jaw stiffened. "I guess that remains to be seen."

"Yes, of course," the queen said with a

condescending smile. "Now, drop your weapons."

My eyes went to Gavril, but his guarded expression made it absolutely impossible to guess what he was thinking. If the prince thing doesn't work out for him, he should definitely consider a career as a professional poker player.

"I said DROP YOUR WEAPONS!"

Gavril hesitated for another long moment. Then, he stooped and placed his sword on the stone floor. The rest of us followed his lead. I mean, what else could we do? I did mention that we were surrounded by two squads of *armed* soldiers, right?

The queen smiled again, looking as smug as Kat did the last time she beat me at checkers, and turned to her men. "Seize them."

Before I could react, a soldier roughly grabbed me by the back of my shirt and started pushing me down the passageway.

"Hey! Let me go!"

I twisted my body, trying to pull away from him, but I swear the guy's hands were coated with Super Glue or something. I just couldn't break free.

The queen dragged us (literally) through the castle without pointing out a single thing or saying a single word, making her the world's worst tour guide. Then, she led us down a dark, circular flight of stairs into the dungeon!

Yep, she was also the world's worst hostess.

The passageway we entered at the bottom of the stairs was lined on both sides with heavy, wooden doors set deep into the stone walls. A few pathetic-looking torches hung here and there on the walls, barely lifting the darkness.

"Man, this is bad," Ron said.

I found myself agreeing with him.

The deeper we went into the dungeon, the worse things looked for us. I could hear moans and groans coming from some of the cells. As we passed one door, a pair of hands snaked out through a small, barred window and grabbed ahold of Gavril.

"Prince Gavril!" the owner of the hands said. "How have you come to this terrible place?"

I couldn't see the guy's face, but his voice sounded so familiar.

"Erick the Huntsman!" Gavril said, grasping the man's hand.

Wait a minute...

Erick the Huntsman... Erick the Hunter.

"Erick Hunter!" I yelled.

My missing stepdad!

I pulled away from Mr. Super Glue and threw myself at the cell door. "You're here! I knew you didn't leave us for some woman. I knew it!"

Gavril stepped back as Ron and Kat joined me at the door. They were just as excited as I was. As for Erick, he seemed stunned.

"Ron? Kat? Timmy? I can't believe it. What are you three doing here?"

"ENOUGH!" The queen said with a lift of her hand. "You've had your little reunion. Now get moving."

"No!" I tried to turn back as the soldiers forced me on. "Erick!"

"Gavril," I heard Erick shout as we were pushed down the corridor. "Protect them. And get them away from here!"

His words were drowned out by a loud screech. A guard had opened a cell door just a short distance down the corridor and was waiting there for us, key in hand.

I wish I could say we put up a gallant fight, subdued our guards, and locked them with the queen into the cell they meant for us.

But that would be lying.

The truth is, it was ridiculously easy for the soldiers to push us into that dungeon cell. Thrown off balance, I landed on the stone floor, partially on top of someone else.

"Get off me!" that person said, giving me a shove.

Yeah, it was Kat.

I scrambled to my feet and looked back toward the doorway. The queen stood there, outlined by the glow of the torches behind her.

"Enjoy the rats," she said with a soft laugh.

Rats?

Before any of us had a chance to respond, the door swung shut, the key turned in the lock, and we were left in total darkness.

Well, almost total darkness. If you looked closely enough, you could just see a glimmer of light through the small barred section of the door. But it did little to improve upon our circumstances.

"No!" Kat screamed.

I wasn't sure if she was more upset about the rats or the dark cell. For me, it was a toss-up.

"Is everyone okay?" Gavril said.

"We're locked in a dungeon with rats," Kat said. "Does that sound okay to you?"

Not to me.

"Maybe she was kidding about the rats," I said hopefully.

"She wasn't," Beriman said.

That's all Kat needed to hear. "We've got to get out of here!"

"Nobody panic," Gavril said. "Just let me check the door."

"I can do it," Ron said. And then he immediately stepped on my hand.

"Ow! Will you watch where you're going?"

"Sorry, Timmy. I can't see a thing."

"You could always light a match," I said, rubbing my injured fingers.

"Oh, yeah! I forgot about them."

Moments later, a match flared in Ron's hand, and he made it to the door without stepping on anyone else. But when he got there, he sounded surprised.

"Hey, there's no handle on this thing! Just a keyhole. We're not getting out this way."

"Don't worry," Gavril said. "We'll think of something. But for now, I suggest we all try to get some rest."

"Are you kidding me?" Kat said, panic rising in her voice again. "And have the rats eat my face while I'm sleeping? I don't think so."

"Rats are not going to eat your face," Ron said.

"They might," Beriman said.

"Then I'm not sleeping either," Ron said.

"Fine," Gavril said. "Don't sleep. Just be quiet so I can get some rest."

"No," Kat said. "Not until you clear something up."

Gavril sighed. He seemed to do a lot of that. "What?"

"Why didn't you tell us that the queen is your

stepmother?"

"I thought we *did* tell you."

"No, you didn't," Kat said. "I distinctly remember the king saying that Queen Morissa overthrew his kingdom. But he neglected to mention the queen was his wife!"

"Yeah," Ron said. "I thought she was a crazy lady from the kingdom next door or something."

"I'm sorry," Gavril said. "I assumed you knew."

"Well, we didn't," Kat said, obviously still ticked off.

Everyone fell silent. I could hear water dripping somewhere in the cell. And I swear I heard the pitter-patter of what was probably rats' feet on the stone floor.

Not good.

"Gavril, how did Queen Morissa get the magic mirror in the first place?" I asked, trying to keep my mind off the rats.

"I'm not sure," said Gavril. "When Morissa married my father and moved into the castle, the mirror came with her."

"Did you know it was magic?" Kat asked.

I could imagine Gavril shrugging in the darkness. "Sure but we had no idea of its true power. We just thought she was using it to compare her beauty to the other ladies in the land. She is quite vain, you know."

"Mirror, mirror on the wall. Who's the fairest of them all?" Kat murmured.

"Something like that," said Gavril. "Our first sign of trouble was when Arianna, my sister, turned eighteen years old. It's too long a story to get into here, but Morissa tried to kill her. And, if it wasn't for Erick the Huntsman, she would have succeeded."

"So what happened?" Ron asked.

"Ron, you know what happened," Kat said.

"No, I don't."

"Yes, you do. Arianna was saved by true love's kiss, married her prince, and lived happily ever after." Kat paused to catch her breath and then asked: "Am I right, Gavril?"

"For the most part, yes. But how did you know?"

"The Brothers Grimm wrote about it in a story called *Snow White*."

Gavril laughed. "Well, that explains a lot! They were here when Morissa went after Arianna. They were constantly asking questions and getting in my way. So that's what they were doing. They were trying to write a story!"

"Well, they didn't write about the part where Queen Morissa takes over your kingdom," Kat said. "How did that happen?"

Gavril grew quiet for a moment. Finally, he said: "The king and I had traveled with some of our men to the kingdom of Folkestone in the north country, where Arianna and her husband rule. It was my nephew's christening."

"You should have never left the queen alone in the castle," Beriman said.

"Yes, we know that now," Gavril said.

"Well, what happened?" Ron asked.

"While we were gone, Queen Morissa turned the hearts of the men we had left at the castle against us. She does have her charms, you know."

"Oh, I've noticed," Ron said.

Gavril gave a little laugh. "Half of the soldiers

are in love with her. The other half are terrified of her. Either way, they would eagerly do as she commanded. So, it was easy for her to use the information she got from the mirror to set an ambush for us."

Gavril paused for a moment and then added quietly: "We never saw it coming."

Silence. For once, I didn't know what to say.

"If we have any hope of getting my kingdom back," Gavril said, "we need to get the mirror. If we don't retrieve it, the queen will always be one step ahead of us."

"I think you're forgetting something, Gavril," Beriman said. "We're locked in a dungeon. And the queen will probably kill us in the morning."

"Over my dead body!" I said.

Okay, that came out wrong, but I knew one thing.

We had to escape — or die trying.

The Great Wizard to the Rescue

I was hoping things would look better when morning came, but they didn't.

Some light did manage to come in through a small, barred window that was set high up in the outside wall. But it only showed us how awful things really were.

There were no secret escape tunnels in the walls. No hidden trap doors in the floor. All I could see were four solid stone walls, an equally solid wooden door, and a window that was only large enough for a gerbil to fit through.

No way out.

It was downright depressing. I know I should have been glad we made it through the night without being eaten alive by rats. But that wasn't enough to make me feel better.

I cheered up a bit, though, when I realized we still had our packs.

"I'm glad they didn't take our food," I said, rummaging through my pack and tossing pieces of deer jerky and dried fruit to everyone.

"We'd better go sparingly with the food and water," Gavril said. "We don't know how long we're going to be in here."

"We need to get out of here today," Kat said. "I'm not spending another night in this place."

"I'm open to any ideas," Gavril said.

Silence. You could hear crickets chirping.

For real.

To keep myself occupied, I continued to dig through the pack. I know it sounds stupid, but I was hoping to discover a forgotten candy bar or even just a stick of gum hiding inside. That's the kind of stuff I always find in my backpack at home.

"I've got it!" I shouted.

Gavril whipped around. "What? A plan?"

"No, my PlayStation." I held it up for them all to see. "I just found it in the bottom of the pack. I'd forgotten all about it."

"Great," Kat said, rolling her eyes. "That's a big help."

Beriman craned his neck to see. "What does he have there?"

"Oh, it's just a stupid video game," Ron said.

Beriman gave him a look that plainly said he did not know what Ron was talking about — which, of course, he didn't. But that didn't faze my big brother in the least.

"He used to play it all the time. Maybe we'll be lucky and the batteries will have run down."

I hit the "on" button. "Cool, it still works!"

"Then again," Ron said, "maybe not."

"Timmy, we're trying to think of a way out of here," Kat said.

I pushed a button to select a game to play. "Go right ahead. I'm listening."

Kat sat down with a sigh and said to the others: "Once he starts playing that stupid thing, Timmy will be no help at all. Not that he's much help anyway."

"I heard that."

"Let's just focus, okay?" Gavril said. "We need to come up with an escape plan."

"If only we had some kind of weapon," Beriman said. "Then we could overpower the guards when they come in here with food. Of course," he added, "that's assuming they feed us."

"Wait!" Ron said. "I've *got* a weapon!"

I looked up from shooting aliens to see him fishing through his pockets and pulling out his Swiss Army knife.

Beriman's eyebrows shot up. "What is that?"

"It's a knife, of course," he said, opening the largest blade.

Beriman took it from him and examined it. He gave a snort. "You call that a weapon? Look how short the blade is."

Ron snatched it back. "Well, it has other parts, too, you know."

Totally distracted from my game, I watched as he began pulling out each tool as he named it: "A bottle-opener, a screwdriver, a corkscrew, and a pair of tweezers. See?"

"What are we supposed to do, Ron?" Kat said. "Threaten to tweeze the guards' eyebrows unless they let us go?"

I laughed. "Did you see the dude with the unibrow? We'd be doing him a favor!"

Ron shoved the knife back into his pocket. "Well, we've got to try something. What about your dagger, Gavril? Do you still have it?"

"No, the soldiers took it. But it's no match for a

sword anyway. You have to be very near your opponent to use it effectively. No decent swordsman is going to let you get that close."

"What we need is a bazooka," I said, turning my attention (mostly) back on the invading aliens in my PlayStation.

"Oh, this is hopeless!" Kat said. "We're never going to get out of here!"

"Kat, remember when our football team needed two touchdowns to win, and our running back had to be carried off the field because he had broken a rib?"

"Ron, please! No football stories!"

"Hey, I was only trying to help!"

"You know what would help?" Kat said. "Timmy turning off that dumb game. It's making so much noise I can't think!"

"You can't think anyway," I said without looking up.

"Why you little—"

"Take it easy, Kat," Ron said. "Timmy, will you please turn down the volume on that thing?"

I sighed and turned off the sound. "Happy now?"

The resulting silence in the room would have been deafening if it wasn't for the noises in the passageway.

Wait — *noises?*

I could hear the rattle of a key turning in a lock. Someone was at the door. We all looked at each other and then turned and stared at the door as it slowly scraped open.

Two soldiers stepped in. One was carrying a tray, and the other was holding a sword. But I barely had time to spare them a glance. The aliens chose that moment to pulverize one of my ships.

"No!" I said, getting back into my game.

Now, you're probably thinking I should have been paying attention to what was going on in the cell. I was. Really! I'm totally able to do two things at once. (It's a gift.)

So when everyone (except me) leapt to their feet to confront the soldiers, I saw it perfectly well.

And I saw (and heard) when the nastier of the two soldiers pressed the point of his sword against Gavril's chest and said: "Stay back, Gavril."

Surprisingly, Gavril lifted his hands and smiled. He seemed about as threatening as a kitten. "Seaton, my old friend," he said. "Why don't you put the sword down?"

Seaton backed up a step, but kept his sword high. "You are an enemy of the queen. You are not my friend."

"What loyalty," Gavril said. "I'm sure the queen will reward you. In fact," he added, "it looks like she already has. Isn't that my dagger you're wearing?"

Seaton smiled, revealing two rows of yellow, crooked teeth. "It is. The queen gave it to me. I'm one of her favorites now."

I glanced up just in time to see Gavril's jaw tighten a bit. His right hand formed a fist, but he somehow managed to scrape up enough self-control to not hit the guy.

Instead, he looked at the soldier holding the tray. "Hello, Jedrek."

"I've brought your breakfast," Jedrek muttered, avoiding his eyes.

"Jedrek, put the tray down and go guard the

door," Seaton said.

The soldier obediently put the tray on the floor and moved away.

"You're just feeding us bread and water?" Ron said. "Are you serious?"

"The bread's probably stale," said Beriman.

"How are we supposed to survive on stale bread?" Kat asked.

"I wouldn't worry about that. You're not going to be in here long enough to starve to death," said Seaton.

Beriman stepped up to him, his beard bristling. "Perhaps you'd like to explain what you mean by that? What exactly is the queen planning on doing with us?"

"Back off, dwarf!" Seaton said, raising his sword. "Sit back down on the floor, all of you!"

"No," said Gavril. "We'll remain standing."

"Then you leave me no choice," Seaton said.

I looked up again to see Seaton lunging at Gavril with his sword.

"Gavril, look out!" I shouted.

Gavril dodged the sword, while somehow managing to push Kat to safety behind him.

Impressive to be sure. But what happened next was so mind-blowing that it made me momentarily forget all about my video game.

Beriman and Ron — yes, *Ron* — stepped in between Gavril and Seaton. Ron had his Swiss Army knife out, as if it were a sword or dagger. (And you already know how *unlike* a sword a Swiss Army knife is!)

I held my breath — afraid I was about to witness the only battle ever fought with a pocketknife —

when from out of nowhere came a blood-curdling scream.

Everyone jumped, including Seaton. I noticed Jedrek cowering near me, his face as white as a sheet. It was obvious that he was the one who had screamed. But why?

And why was he pointing at me?

"Timmy, what have you done?" Kat asked, assuming the worst of me, as usual.

"Nothing!" I looked down at the video game in my hands. Great. The aliens were still attacking, and I was getting clobbered.

"It's magic," Jedrek finally said, still pointing at me with a shaky finger. "There are people in that box! Little people!"

"What? In this?" I scrambled to my feet and walked toward him, holding out the game.

"Keep it away from me," Jedrek said, backing up. "Keep it away!"

I stopped, confused.

"Let me see that." Seaton said. Pushing past Gavril, he grabbed me by the arm and yanked me around.

"Hey! That hurt!"

Seaton ignored me. He just froze in place, staring at my game.

"It is true! There are people in there!" He dropped my arm like it burned him and backed away from me. "He's a wizard! A great wizard!"

"Timmy, a wizard?" Ron said with a laugh. "Man, are you making a mistake!"

Gavril quickly stepped in front of him. "That's right, Seaton. You're making a huge mistake. You've thrown a wizard into a dungeon. You are very fortunate that he hasn't shrunk you like he has shrunk the others."

"That's right," I said. "Wait... what?"

"But I don't know how long I can hold the wizard off," Gavril said to the soldiers. "I think you'd better hand over your weapons. Now!"

Jedrek's sword clattered to the floor. Ron moved in and snatched it up. But Seaton hesitated, staring at me.

"Fine, it's your choice, Seaton," Gavril said with a shrug. "Go ahead and shrink him, Tim."

"No, wait!" Seaton said.

To my amazement, the soldier handed over his sword. Gavril slid it into his empty sheath and held out his hand.

"Now, give me my dagger, if you please," Gavril said. "And the key."

With great reluctance — and with his eyes on me the whole time — Seaton obeyed.

"Grab the packs," Gavril told us. "We're getting out of here."

"You'll regret this, Gavril," Seaton said.

"Not as much as you will when the queen finds you locked in here," Gavril said. "She doesn't tolerate failure well."

Seaton lunged forward at that, but I whipped around and pointed my game at him.

"Go ahead. Make my day."

Trapped!

Of course I couldn't shrink Seaton and hold him captive in my little box (video game) with the other shrunken people (digital aliens).

But Seaton didn't know that, so he (grudgingly) allowed Gavril to lock him and Jedrek into the dungeon cell.

I'll never forget the expression on his face as that door swung shut. He looked mad enough to grow fangs.

Gavril leaned against the wall and gave a low whistle. "I can't believe they fell for that."

"Me neither," Ron said.

I raised my video game high. "Tim the Great Wizard saved the day!"

Kat scoffed. "No, stupid. All you did was play a video game. It was Gavril's quick thinking that saved the day."

"You're just jealous."

"Yeah, well you're delusional!"

"Am not! I really did save us with my video game, didn't I, Gavril?"

But Gavril wasn't listening. He was already down the corridor, unlocking Erick's door.

The man who stepped out of the cell was thinner than I remembered. His dark, wavy hair was longish and shaggy, his beard was scraggly, and his clothes were dirty and torn. But his twinkling blue eyes were the same.

"Erick!" I said, rushing him with a bear hug.

Kat and Ron had the same idea — at the same time. The force of our greeting almost knocked Erick over, but he just grinned.

"You don't know how good it is to see you three," he said, hugging us back. "But what are you doing here?"

"What are *you* doing here?" Kat asked.

"This used to be my home," Erick said.

"What?" Ron said. "The dungeon?"

"No," Erick laughed. "This kingdom."

"Wait," Kat said. "I don't understand."

Gavril cut her off. "I hate to break this up, but we don't have time for a reunion right now."

"You're right," Erick said. "We need to get these three out of here and back home. Their mother must be very worried about them."

"Not before we get the mirror," Gavril said.

"The mirror? Is that what you're after?" Erick shook his head. "It's far too dangerous. You should be here with a troop of your best soldiers — not three kids from Connecticut."

"I would be inclined to agree with you," Gavril said. "But the king believes they are the three mentioned in the prophecy."

Erick's jaw dropped. "The ones that are supposed to deliver us from the evil queen?" He took Gavril aside and lowered his voice. "Don't get me wrong. I love these kids. But I wouldn't trust them to deliver a pizza."

Funny. I had thought the same thing.

"We heard that," Kat said. "Thanks for the vote

of confidence, Erick."

"I just don't want anything to happen to you."

Gavril looked impatient. "We can't have this conversation right now. We have to get to the mirror before the queen knows we've escaped. Who's with me?"

"I'm in," Ron said.

"So am I," Beriman said.

"Me too," Kat and I said at the same time.

Erick hesitated, staring at us. "If anything happens to you three, your mom will kill me."

Ron shrugged. "We're just taking a mirror. How hard can it be?"

Erick sighed. "Fine. Let's do this thing."

Gavril immediately sprang into action. We almost had to run to keep up with him as he led the way up the stairs. He paused at the top only long enough to see if the way was clear — and then it was off to the races again.

We went as quickly and as quietly as possible down one corridor after another and dashed up a long flight of stairs. We had to duck into doorways a couple of times to avoid patrolling soldiers, but somehow we made it to the second floor without anyone spotting us.

"This way," Gavril whispered, heading down yet another passageway. Near the end, he stopped before a fancy wooden door and listened.

And listened.

"What are we waiting for?" I whispered after what seemed like an eternity.

Gavril silenced me with a look. Slowly, he pushed the door open and poked his head inside. After a quick look around, he stepped through the doorway and motioned for us to follow. We scurried into the room and shut the door behind us.

"The queen's sitting room," Erick whispered.

"Wow," I whispered back.

The room had a huge stone fireplace, hanging tapestries, and fancy wooden furniture. A set of glass doors led out to a large balcony that had a view of the gardens. I especially liked the dark red curtains that hung on either side of them. They were trimmed with a gold cord that made them look extra special and expensive.

Gavril didn't look around the room at all. He just hurried over to a closed door on the far wall and pressed his ear against it.

The strangest expression crossed his face.

Motioning for us to be quiet, he carefully pulled the door open just enough to peek in.

We crowded around him, straining to see. I could just make out the queen, standing in what looked like a bedroom. I couldn't see anyone else in the room with her.

"Here's to victory," she said, raising the golden cup in her hand. "And here's to King Gunther, the fool."

She took a big sip and laughed. Then she continued to carry on a conversation with (apparently) herself.

"Imagine sending Gavril, a dwarf, and those three idiots to defeat me," she said, "all because he's stupid enough to believe some old prophecy."

Queen Morissa laughed again, as if she had just said something funny — which, by the way, she didn't.

"And now they're languishing away in my

dungeon." She paused. "Or, are they? Gavril is smart — and tricky."

She whirled around, turning her back to us, and spoke: "Mirror, mirror, please do tell," she said. "Show me my enemies inside their cell."

There was a long pause, and I heard the queen give a little gasp. "Impossible!"

She slammed her cup down on a small table, causing dark red liquid to splash out of it. "Heads will roll for this!"

Then, the queen pushed herself away from the table and disappeared from our sight.

A door slammed and there was the sound of quick footsteps in the corridor. "Guards! Guards!"

As the queen's cries faded, Gavril pushed open the door to her bedroom. "Okay, come on. We need to make this quick."

We crowded into the room, but I quickly forgot about finding the mirror.

"Look at that bed!" I said.

It sat in the center of the room, wrapped in a canopy of velvet curtains that stretched from floor to ceiling. It was so big it could sleep a family of five and two Dobermans with room to spare.

I had to fight the sudden urge to jump on it.

"Everyone, over here," Erick said.

Both Gavril and Erick were standing by a stone fireplace, staring at something that hung over it.

The mirror.

Wow!

The sunlight coming through the window shone right on it, making my first glimpse of the mirror something special. Its gold frame — carved with animals, birds, and flowers — gleamed. And its jewels sparkled.

Yes, you read that right. It was embedded with jewels. Dozens of them!

It. Was. Amazing.

Kat practically cooed. "It's so beautiful."

"Are those jewels real?" I asked.

"No one look into it," Gavril said, snatching the mirror off the wall and wrapping it in a velvet cloth he had pulled off the bed.

"Why?" I asked.

Gavril glanced up from securing the cloth. "Because it draws you in somehow. Everyone who looks in it becomes obsessed with it. It's like they're bewitched or something."

"Weird."

Erick had moved over to the door that presumably led out into the hallway. "Gavril, are you about ready? We need to get out of here."

"Right." Gavril tucked the wrapped mirror under his arm. "Let's go."

"What's the big rush?" Ron asked while stifling a yawn.

He was eying the bed. He probably wanted a nap.

"The queen saw the empty cell in the mirror," Gavril said, joining Erick at the door. "She knows we've escaped."

Ron instantly seemed more awake. "Really? Well, what are we waiting for? We need to get out of here!"

Gavril gave him a look that plainly said "ya think?" and cracked the door to the corridor. He quickly shut it again.

"Into the sitting room! Now!"

I had never heard Gavril sound so urgent. Apparently, the others hadn't either. We obeyed instantly, scrambling over each other to make it into the next room as quickly as possible. And it was a good thing we did.

Just as we reached the sitting room, the bedroom door burst open and the queen hurried in from the corridor. I caught a brief glimpse of soldiers swarming into the room after her before Gavril quickly shut the door between us.

"I'll ask the mirror where they are," I heard the queen say to the soldiers. "And when we find them, I want them dead."

But half a heartbeat later, a horrible cry filled the air.

Uh-oh...

"My mirror! They've taken my mirror!"

Shoot. I was hoping we'd be farther away before she discovered it missing.

Like home. In Connecticut.

"They couldn't have gotten far," a soldier said. "We will find them, my queen. We will get your mirror back."

"This is all my fault," the queen said, sounding worried. "When I discovered those brats missing from the dungeon, I should have asked the mirror where they were. I lost my head. They must have been close by when I left the room to get you."

The queen gave a gasp. "The sitting room! Check the sitting room!"

Gavril threw his weight against the door just as it started to open.

"Erick, help me!" he yelled. "Everyone else, get something to block both doors!"

Ron and Beriman dragged a large cabinet in front of the bedroom door, while Kat and I lugged a heavy bench over to the other door that led to the corridor.

"Gavril," the queen said from the bedroom. "Open this door and give me back my mirror, and I will let you live. Otherwise, you will all die. You have two minutes to decide!"

Two minutes, and then we die? Not good.

"What are we going to do?" I asked.

"I'm thinking," Gavril said.

Thinking?

"We can't wait, Gavril," Ron said. "We need to destroy the mirror now!"

"Ron, no," Gavril started to say, but Ron wasn't listening. He snatched up the mirror, ripped off the velvet covering, and slammed it with all his strength against the stone fireplace.

A brilliant light exploded into the room with a force of a fireball, lifting Ron off his feet and sending him crashing into the nearby wall.

"Ron!" Kat screamed.

But my brother just lay there, not moving.

Caught in the Maze

We all rushed over to Ron.

He groaned and stirred as we reached him.

"Ron, are you okay?" I asked.

My brother shook his head slightly — like he was trying to clear it — and started pushing himself up.

Erick grabbed ahold of him. "Take it easy, Ron. You've had a shock."

"No kidding. I felt like I was hit by a bolt of lightning or something. It was insane."

"Are you hurt?" Gavril asked.

"Nah," Ron said, slowly getting to his feet. "Just a bit banged up. I'll survive. How about the mirror? Did I destroy it?"

We all looked at where the mirror lay face up on the floor.

"You didn't even scratch it!" I said.

"Great."

Gavril picked up the mirror and began replacing the velvet cloth. "Ron, why do you think we're taking it back to Fenimore Castle? We can only destroy the mirror on Dragon Rock, remember?"

"Oh, yeah."

"Uh, we're running out of time, people," Beriman said. "We need to find a way out of here — and now."

"Agreed," Gavril said. "Let's try the balcony."

We followed him out of the glass doors and crowded around the balcony railing.

"It's got to be a forty foot drop," Kat said. "What are we going to do? Fly?"

"Maybe we can climb down," Gavril said.

Kat frowned. "Did you bring any rope?"

Gavril looked a little embarrassed. "Just what's wrapped around the packs."

Kat frowned deeper. "That's too short."

"Then we're stuck here," Beriman said. "And the queen will break down the door and kill us all."

Gavril rubbed his forehead like he was getting a headache, which he probably was. "Not helping, Beriman."

"But Gavril, he's right," Kat said. "If we don't get off this balcony now, we're all going to die! And we'll never get home. And Mom and Grandma will never know what happened to us!"

"I've got an idea," Ron said.

Kat, Erick, and I turned as one to stare at him. Ron hardly ever had ideas. Well, not ones that he made public, anyway. And the few ideas he did have usually weren't very good unless they involved football.

"What is it?" Gavril asked.

"Why don't we use that gold rope on the curtains to climb down from the balcony?"

A light came on in Gavril's eyes. "Well done, Ron! Why didn't I think of that?"

We hurried back into the sitting room and examined the thick cord that trimmed the drapes.

Gavril smiled. "Yes, this could work."

My heart leaped. We had a plan! We were

getting out of there!

"Your time is up, Gavril," came the queen's voice through the door. "We're coming in!"

My heart sank. Our plan came too late.

As if on cue, something hard hit both doors at the same time, making them shudder — and making me jump. And the sound came again and again.

Yep, you guessed it. They were breaking down the doors — just like the queen said they would.

Awesome.

"We don't have much time," Gavril said. "Help me get these curtains down."

All it took was a couple of good, strong yanks from Erick, and we had access to all the gold cord we wanted. We stripped it off the curtains in record time, and Gavril tied several lengths together with some secure-looking knots.

At least, I hoped they were secure. Beriman seemed doubtful.

"Do you really think it's strong enough to hold us?" he asked, tugging at it.

Gavril took it from his hands. "We'll have to take that chance. Those doors are going to give way at any moment, and we don't want to be here when they do."

Out on the balcony, Gavril secured one end of the rope to the stone railing and tossed the other over the side.

"Ron, you go first."

With a grin, Ron swung himself over the railing and scampered down the rope like a monkey down a tree.

Yep. Mr. Athlete was nearly electrocuted to death by the mirror, but he still managed to nail rappelling on his first try.

Surprised? Me neither.

Kat went next, followed by Erick and Beriman. That left me and Gavril alone on the balcony.

Gavril handed me the rope. "Tim, get going."

I eased my legs over the balcony and started down. I tried my best to imitate Ron's rappelling technique, but I ended up bouncing my way down the castle wall like a bunny on steroids.

Yeah, it wasn't pretty. But at least I made it in one piece.

Suddenly, there was a loud crash.

"The doors!" Gavril shouted. "They've broken through!"

He swung his legs over the railing, grasping the rope in one hand and clutching the mirror under his other arm.

Gavril had barely started down when Queen Morissa appeared on the balcony, surrounded by her ever-devoted soldiers.

She looked over the railing and took about one second to study the situation. "You," she said to the soldier standing next to her. "Go after him!"

"Gavril, hurry!" I yelled.

"I'm going as fast as I can!"

"The mirror is slowing him down," Erick said, dashing to stand underneath him. "Gavril, drop the mirror! I'll catch it."

Gavril didn't hesitate. He let go of the mirror and began to move so fast that he was practically sliding down the rope.

"Come on, Gavril!" Ron yelled.

Gavril released the rope and fell the remaining fifteen feet or so. He landed with an expert-looking roll and leapt to his feet.

"Run!" he said.

The queen let out another one of those horrible cries. "They must not get away! After them!"

A Quick Retreat

Boy, was she ticked!

I think Gavril's done this before

←The Mirror

This was much harder than it looks

Let me tell you... we ran through that garden like six scared rabbits being chased by a pack of starving wolves.

We plowed through large, colorful flower beds, zipped past flowing fountains, and dodged a few bushes trimmed in the shapes of horses and elephants.

It was so cool. I wished I had time to look around. But, I didn't. If you had an evil queen and hordes of nasty soldiers after you, you wouldn't want to stay and check out the scenery either.

After running for what felt like hours — it was probably more like three minutes — we stopped to catch our breath beside a tall, thick hedge. But we didn't get much of a break.

"They're coming," Kat said between pants.

I looked in the direction her finger was pointing. Sure enough, a troop of soldiers was rounding the side of the castle and spilling into the gardens like an army of ants in search of a picnic.

Unfortunately, the hedge was blocking our escape route. We ran alongside it, looking for a way around.

I was the first one to spot an opening. "In here!" I said, darting through it.

I found myself in a narrow, grassy pathway between two tall hedges. Something about it felt very odd to me, but I kept running anyway.

"Stop!" Gavril yelled from somewhere behind me. "Everyone stop!"

I obeyed instantly, sending clods of grass and dirt flying. Ron and Kat, who were following close behind, slammed into me and knocked me to the ground.

Ron helped me up. "Sorry, Timmy."

"I wish you guys would stop doing that."

Gavril ran up with Erick and Beriman. He was holding the mirror again.

Somehow he had managed to get it from Erick. While running. They probably passed it like those guys pass batons in relay races.

It would have been cool to watch them do that. I wished I hadn't missed it.

"We've got to go back," Gavril said.

"What are you talking about?" I asked. "There are soldiers back there. With weapons. Chasing us."

"You've led us into a maze."

"Really, Gavril? Cool!"

I had heard about those hedge mazes that castles used to have. I had always wanted to try one out.

"Not cool," Gavril said. "There's only one way in and one way out."

"So?"

"So, all the soldiers have to do is guard the entrance and exit and wait for us to come out."

Kat looked horrified. "So you're saying we're trapped? Again?"

"If we don't get out of here right now, we will be."

"Then let's get out of here," Beriman said, taking off in the direction we had come.

It took us mere seconds to get back to the maze entrance, but one look told us we were too late.

The soldiers were nearly upon us — led by the queen herself.

Gavril looked grim, which was nothing new. "Okay, we'll have to take our chances with the maze."

"Way to go, Timmy," Kat said.

"How was I supposed to know?"

"Everyone, follow me," Gavril said, cutting off what was sure to be a mean response from Kat.

Gavril led the way down one maze passageway after another, taking the twists and turns without any hesitation at all.

"He really seems to know where he's going," I said to Erick as I jogged to keep up.

"He does. He grew up here, remember? He and Arianna spent many hours playing in this maze."

Beriman snorted. "I don't see what good that does us. We already know what will be waiting for us when we find our way out of here."

"Have courage, my friend," Gavril said.

He kept looking up at the sun, as if trying to judge the direction we were headed. Finally, he stopped in front of a section of the maze.

"If I'm correct," Gavril said, "this is the back of the maze. Beyond this hedge is an open field and then some woods."

"And no soldiers," Erick said, "because they'll be waiting for us at the exit."

Gavril nodded. "Right. All we need to do is break through the hedge."

"How are we supposed to do that?" Ron asked.

"Like this."

Tossing aside the mirror, Gavril drew his sword and began to hack away at the lower branches. Ron, who was the only other one with a weapon, quickly joined him. But the hedge was thick, and even I could see that swords were the wrong tool for the job.

I wished I had thought to bring along some

hedge clippers.

Kat looked worried. "Shouldn't we be keeping watch for soldiers?"

"You're right," Erick said. "I'm on it."

He jogged down to the nearest corner and positioned himself to watch the passageway we had just come up.

I followed him.

"So Erick, did you really used to live here?"

Erick glanced at me. "Yeah. I had a small cottage right here on the castle grounds."

"Why did you want to leave?"

Seriously, if I could live in a place that had both a castle and a hedge maze, not even a team of mafia assassins would be able to get me out of there.

"I had no choice," Erick said, one eye still on the passageway. "The queen wanted me to kill Arianna for her. I disobeyed and became a marked man. I went through the mirror to save my life."

"And found yourself in Connecticut."

Erick grinned. "Right. I had stepped out of a mirror in an antique store. I traded my gold watch for the mirror because I had some vague idea of returning home someday."

"But then you met Mom."

"Yeah, I met your mother, and it changed everything. But you need to know something, Timmy," Erick said, giving me his full attention. "It was wrong of me to leave here when I did. I know how to fight. I should have stayed and helped Gavril."

"Is that why you went back through the mirror?"

"Yes. I wanted to make sure everyone was okay.

But when I arrived, the king and Gavril were up north, and Queen Morissa was solidifying her power at Tryton. It wasn't long before I was captured by the queen's soldiers and thrown into the dungeon."

"That explains a lot. We were just so worried about you."

"I know, Timmy. And I'm sorry I disappeared like I did. I never would have willingly left all of you. I love you guys."

"Yeah, I know. I just thought—"

I stopped mid-sentence when Erick grabbed my shoulder. "What? What is it?"

I turned to look down the passageway.

Soldiers! They had just come around the far corner of the maze and were headed right for us.

Erick gave me a push. "Go, go!"

We ran back to the others. Erick reached them first.

"Soldiers!"

"What?" said Gavril. "How close?"

"Very," Erick said. "We have to get out of here now."

"Okay." Gavril looked at me. "Through the hedge, Tim."

I looked at the hole they had made. Frankly, it seemed a bit small.

"Tim, now!"

I dropped to my knees and began to push my way through the hedge. It was only about three feet thick, but don't think for one minute that it was easy going.

The process of making a hole in the hedge left a bunch of freshly-cut branches with razor-sharp ends. I got scratched up something awful and tore my shorts.

"Just great," I said to myself, looking at the damage when I came out on the other side. "They were new, too. Mom is going to kill me."

Beriman came next, pushing the mirror through the hedge in front of him. His beard was full of bits of branches and leaves.

"That hole is too small," he said, picking at his beard.

Yeah, no kidding.

One by one, the others quickly joined us. Everyone had some scratches, rips in their clothing, and leaves in their hair. But at least we were still ahead of the soldiers.

Gavril, who was the last one through, took the mirror from Beriman and said: "Come on. Let's get out of here."

"Wait!" Ron said. "I left my pack in the maze."

Now you may be thinking: *So what? Just get out of there!* And I would normally agree with you. But here's the thing...

We had used up quite a bit of our food, so we were down to just two packs — one carried by Gavril and the other by Ron.

"Ron!" Kat said. "Most of our food is in that pack!"

"And my video game!" I said. "It saved our lives! I won't leave it behind!"

Without thinking, I dove back into the hole in the hedge. I could hear the others' cries as they tried to stop me, but I kept going anyway.

I needed to get that video game back.

It wasn't until I burst into the maze that I realized how stupid I was. The soldiers were close —

just about ten feet away.

They looked surprised. A couple of them even shouted.

You'd think they never saw a kid pop out of a hedge before.

I quickly located the pack, grabbed it, and dove back into the hole.

This time, I didn't even feel the sharp branches jabbing at me. I thrust the pack through to the other side and squirmed along after it as quickly as I could.

My head cleared the hedge and then my shoulders. Clutching at the green grass, I began to pull myself forward when something caught ahold of my foot.

No! This couldn't be happening!

But it was. Someone — or something — was dragging me back into the maze!

Locked in the Tower

"Help!"

Gavril and Erick lunged toward me. I reached out and tried to grab their outstretched hands.

And missed.

The next thing I knew, leaves were closing in over my head, and I was back in that blasted hedge again.

Desperate, I kicked and struggled against whatever had a death grip on my foot, but I couldn't break free.

I felt more hands grabbing at me. And within moments, I was lying on the grass inside the maze, blinking up at a dozen soldiers.

Awesome.

"On your feet!" one of them ordered, pointing his sword at me.

Yeah, right. I was just dragged *backwards* through a prickly hedge. I was scratched up, sore, scared, and, frankly, I wanted my mommy. If the guy thought I was going to budge a muscle, he was crazy.

"I said, on your feet!" The soldier motioned to two of his buddies who grabbed me by the arms and hauled me up.

Yep, he was definitely crazy.

"Ow! Take it easy! Can't you see I'm hurt?"

The soldiers ignored me. In fact, the two guys

hanging onto me didn't let up their grip on my arms one little bit.

Jerks.

"Highsmith," the crazy soldier said to another, "get us out of here. The queen is waiting."

The soldier called Highsmith nodded and took the lead. As I was pulled along behind him, I couldn't help but notice that he navigated the maze as easily as Gavril. I wondered if he grew up playing in it, too.

It took mere minutes to reach the end. The soldiers pulled me through the opening in the hedge, and I found that we were back in the garden again.

My eyes went instantly to the queen.

Just as Gavril had predicted, she was standing near the exit of the maze with a bunch of her soldiers. And, judging by the scowl on her face, she wasn't in a particularly good mood.

"The mirror," she said, coming forward immediately. "Where is it?"

Mr. Crazy Soldier gave a bow. "I don't know, my queen. But we do have the boy."

"The boy?"

The two soldiers holding me pushed me forward. I stumbled and fell to my knees on the grass — right at her feet.

"The boy," she repeated. I kept my eyes down, but I could feel her studying me.

"Where's my mirror, boy?"

"I don't have it."

"I can see that." Queen Morissa lifted my chin with her finger, her long nail biting into my skin.

"You have one last chance to answer me before you die. Where is my mirror?"

Die? Was she serious?

"Let the boy go!" a voice said.

Gavril!

I leapt to my feet. Gavril was standing about twenty feet away, his hand resting on the hilt of his sword.

Shouting his name, I started to run toward him but got yanked back by one of the soldiers.

"He doesn't know where the mirror is, Morissa," Gavril said, looking remarkably calm for someone so seriously outnumbered.

Color flared in the queen's face. "Hold the boy here," she said to the soldier.

He gave a curt nod and gripped my arm tighter.

"Ouch! You're hurting me! Let me go, you big bully!"

I finished my little speech with a backwards kick into the guy's shin. He cried out in pain and had a few choice words to say that really don't bear repeating here.

"Take it easy, Tim," Gavril said. "I've got this."

But his eyes weren't on me. He was watching the queen as she approached him, looking as wary as a cat around a snake.

"You've caused me a lot of trouble, my son," she said. "But your pathetic attempts to dethrone me have failed. I want my mirror back. Now!"

Gavril displayed his empty hands. "I don't have it," he said, stating the obvious.

"I can see that." Her words became harsh and strangled. "Where is it? Where is my mirror?"

Gavril shrugged. "Gone. With the others."

Queen Morissa glanced around wildly. I have to admit, I looked, too. The gardens around us and the large field that bordered the woods were all empty. Ron, Kat, Erick and Beriman were nowhere to be seen.

I wondered where they went.

"Face it, Morissa," Gavril said, cutting into my thoughts. "Without the mirror, you're finished. So let the boy go. He is of no use to you."

"No use to me?"

The queen turned with a swirl of her skirts to stare at me. Her eyes seemed to bore through my t-shirt and into my soul.

"Oh, you're wrong there, Gavril," she said softly, turning to face him with a hand on my shoulder. "This boy is very valuable — to you and your companions, that is. To get him back, you need to give me something valuable in return."

The queen paused and gave Gavril an absolutely wicked smile before adding...

"The mirror."

Yeah, no surprise there. Still, my heart sank. I knew Gavril wouldn't just hand that thing over. Sure enough, out came his sword.

Holding it in front of him, Gavril swiftly closed the distance between us. Queen Morissa gave a sharp gasp and motioned to the soldier who was holding onto me. He whipped out his sword. But did he point it at Gavril?

Nope.

He pressed the tip right into my back!

"Halt!" the queen said, thrusting out her palm. "Or the boy dies."

Gavril stopped maybe three feet away from us, but kept his sword trained on the queen. "If you kill him, you'll never see your precious mirror again.

Ever."

Morissa studied him for a moment with narrowed eyes, and then she gave a light laugh. "Gavril, my son. There is no need for anyone to die — if you do as I say."

Gavril began to shake his head. But, before he could speak, the queen continued.

"Don't worry. I'll give you plenty of time to round up your little friends and retrieve the mirror. We'll exchange it for the boy tomorrow morning at sunrise on the front lawn of the castle."

Gavril glared at her. "I will not do a deal with you, Morissa."

"Pity. I would reconsider, if I were you. Because, if you do not show up with my mirror, the boy will die."

I really wished she would stop saying that.

With a toss of her bright auburn hair, the queen turned and motioned to her soldiers. "Bring him."

The soldier who was holding onto me immediately began to pull me along after the queen as she headed back to the castle.

"No!" I cried, struggling to pull away. "Gavril, do something!"

But Gavril didn't do anything. He just stood there and let the soldiers drag me away.

He didn't care about what happened to me. All he cared about was that stupid mirror.

The mirror of doom.

Yeah, that was a good name for it.

Because of that stupid mirror, soldiers were dragging me down the corridors of the castle against my will — again.

And I was probably going to be tossed into the

dungeon — again. Only this time, I would be alone and wouldn't even have my video game to keep me company.

Yep, my life stunk like a heap of month-old garbage. And it was all the mirror's fault.

I was so busy feeling sorry for myself that I wasn't paying attention to where we were going until we hit a spiral staircase. It was then that I noticed something important.

We were going *up* the stairs. Up! Not down toward the dungeon like I had expected.

"Where are you taking me?"

No answer. The queen just kept walking up that spiral staircase without missing a beat. It was like I hadn't said a thing.

How rude.

Silently, we went round and round and up and up. We passed by landing after landing that led to long, gloomy-looking corridors, and we didn't stop until we reached what seemed to be the top floor of the castle.

Without a word, the queen led us down the passageway to a door located at the end. When she pulled it open, I saw yet another steep spiral staircase.

Wonderful. More stairs.

"You and you," she said, indicating two of the soldiers with a nod of her head, "bring the boy. The rest of you are dismissed."

Queen Morissa gathered her skirts in her hand and started up. The stairs were so narrow that we had to follow her in single file — with me sandwiched between the two soldiers.

"Keep it moving, boy," the guy behind me said,

giving me a push.

I *was* moving, but you know what? That guy poked at me all the way up that staircase. I was almost relieved to reach the landing at the top of the stairs until, that is, the queen pulled open a thick, wooden door.

"After you," she said, gesturing to me.

Figuring I didn't have much choice, I cautiously scooted by the queen and entered a small, round room. It didn't have much for furniture — just a rug on the floor and a couple of uncomfortable-looking benches. But the views made up for it.

There were windows all around, allowing me to see for miles in every direction. The castle gardens, the mountains we had crossed, the little village, the rolling hills and forests, and even the roof of the castle were all spread out before me, looking golden in the late afternoon sun.

"The views from this tower are magnificent, are they not?" the queen asked.

I jumped. I didn't know she was right behind me. She was like a stealth ninja or something.

"Yeah, nice."

The queen walked around me to stand in front of one of the windows. "It's all mine. Everything you see belongs to me."

"Uh-huh." I took a small step backwards toward the door.

"I know it doesn't look like much," the queen said, gazing out at the scenery. "Tryton is a terribly small kingdom."

"Yep." I took another step back.

"But the kings of the neighboring lands are lazy and stupid. They should be easy to conquer. And then I will be revered as the most beautiful and powerful woman in the world."

"Okie dokie." I stole a glance over my shoulder at the door, hoping the two soldiers had struck up a game of "Old Maid" and wouldn't notice my escape attempt.

No such luck. They were standing at attention and watching me like a cat watches a goldfish.

"And no one will ever again say," the queen continued, her voice soft, "that my sister is better than me."

Huh? She had a sister?

Before I could even explore that thought, the queen whirled around and grabbed ahold of my arm.

I didn't even see her coming until she was on top of me. I told you... she's a medieval stealth ninja woman!

"I need that mirror," she said. "Without it, I am nothing! Do you understand? Nothing!"

Suddenly, I remembered the expression on Gavril's face as I was dragged away. He had looked so determined and sad. And I knew.

"Your mirror is gone. Gavril won't give it back to you. Ever."

It was the truth. But I didn't realize I had said it *out loud* until the queen gave a cry of pure rage and thrust me up against the wall. I hit it so hard that the breath was knocked right out of me.

"The mirror is mine," she hissed, inches from my face. "If that fool Gavril does not return it to me, you will die. Do you understand me?"

Terrified, I managed a nod.

"Good." She shoved me roughly aside, and I tumbled to the stone floor, scraping my hands.

Stepping over me, the queen took a moment to smooth her gown and pat her hair back into place before heading to the doorway.

"Stay on guard," she said to the soldiers as she left the tower room. "No one is allowed in this room, except me. Understand?"

"Yes, your Majesty," one of the soldiers said as they followed her out. The door was pulled shut, and I heard a key turn in the lock.

"I'm counting on you," the queen's muffled voice came through the closed door. "He must not escape."

I pulled myself up to a sitting position and hugged my knees to my chest as silence closed in around me.

Escape?

I sighed. I was locked into a tall tower with no rope. I didn't even have a parachute. And Rapunzel was nowhere in sight.

"Even Houdini couldn't get out of this one," I said to myself.

The Great Escape

A wolf howled, startling me awake.

I blinked in the darkness, wondering for a moment where I was.

And then I remembered.

I was locked in a tower. Alone. And no one was going to do a thing to help me.

I uncurled my body from the hard, wooden bench, feeling stiff, sore, and sorry for myself. Actually, I was surprised I had managed to sleep at all — considering the circumstances.

Pushing myself to my feet, I looked out the window. It was still dark outside, but I could see a slight lightening of the sky in the east.

The sun was starting to rise. It was doomsday. For me.

I knew there was no way Gavril would bring back that mirror. So I was toast. Dead meat. Goners.

I was studying the sky, trying to figure out how much time I had before the soldiers came for me, when I heard a thud outside the door.

I whirled around in a panic. They couldn't be coming for me yet. It was too early!

But apparently they were.

There was another thud.

I held my breath, my eyes riveted to the door.

The awful screech of metal grating against metal

filled the small room. The key. Someone turned the key!

I needed to hide. But where? Under a bench? They'd find me there for sure.

Besides, there was no time. The door scraped open, allowing two dark shadows into the tower room.

Men. One was bigger than the other.

I strained my eyes in the growing light and spotted a glint of chain mail under their hooded capes.

Not just men. Soldiers.

Bummer.

The soldiers walked toward me; their faces completely shadowed by their hoods.

Freaky. It looked like the dudes had NO faces. And if that doesn't get all the hair on your arms to stand on end, nothing will.

I shrank back against the bench, my heart pounding in my ears.

I couldn't let two faceless soldiers take me. I had to get away.

But how?

As I racked my brain for ideas, I suddenly noticed two important things.

The door was open.

And nobody was guarding it.

It was time for Tim Hunter to be a hero.

Without pausing to think about the crazy thing I was about to do, I leapt on top of the bench, gave a rebel yell, and launched myself into the air toward the two men.

I collided with them with such force that it knocked them both off balance, and I clung to them like a monkey all the way down to the floor.

Ka-plunk! They went down so hard I must have knocked the wind out of them.

I couldn't believe it. I did it! I took down two big men singlehandedly!

But I had zero time to congratulate myself. My clever maneuver had brought me within five feet of the doorway, and I had some escaping to do.

I started crawling off the men toward freedom, but I didn't get far before the biggest soldier latched onto my leg.

"Let me go!" I cried, kicking at the guy with my free foot.

The man threw up a hand to protect himself. "Timmy, stop it! STOP IT!"

I paused mid-kick. "Erick?"

"Yes," he said, sounding relieved that I was no longer kicking him. "And Gavril is with me."

"Gavril?"

He came for me! He didn't abandon me after all! I suddenly wanted to cry, but I didn't. I was too old for that kind of stuff.

"I thought you were soldiers!" I said instead. "What are you doing here? I thought you would be long gone by now."

"You thought we would abandon you?" Erick asked. "Why would you think that?"

"Well, Gavril didn't even try to stop the queen from taking me. And you and the others weren't even there. I thought you guys didn't care."

"Tim, if we had tried to stop the queen by force," Gavril said, getting to his feet, "she would have killed you on the spot."

"Oh."

He reached down to pull me up and pushed something soft into my hands. "Here, put this on. Quickly."

"What is it?" I asked as I pulled the long tunic over my head.

"A disguise. And you'll need this." Gavril pulled some kind of hat onto my head and over my ears.

Curious, I felt it. Was that a ruffle?

Erick gave me a pat on the back. "Come on, young lady, let's get out of here."

Huh?

Gavril was way ahead of us, as always. "Watch your step," he called from the landing.

Watch my step?

I went to the doorway and was surprised to see two soldiers lying on the landing, half-propped up against the wall.

"What happened to these guys?"

"They wouldn't let us pass," Gavril said simply.

Well, that explained the noises I heard.

I wanted to ask more questions, but Gavril was already heading down the stairs.

"Come on," he called over his shoulder.

Erick and I picked our way over the two men and followed him. When we reached the floor below, Gavril scooped up a bucket from outside a door in the corridor and shoved it into my hands.

"Follow behind us a couple of steps and keep your head down," he said.

I obeyed, but I was totally confused. Why was I carrying a bucket? Why was there a ruffle on my hat? And why had no one noticed us? There were plenty of people around, but no one was giving us a second glance. I could see them overlooking a couple of hooded soldiers like Gavril and Erick, but me?

I'm Tim Hunter, important prisoner. How could they not see me?

That's when I saw another beige-colored tunic and ruffled hat in the passageway — and understood.

It was being worn by a girl.

A girl!

They disguised me as a girl! That was so not funny.

The Great Escape

soldier

Me in my disguise
(no comments, please)

Erick

Gavril

After that embarrassing discovery, I had no trouble keeping my head down. I didn't want anyone to see me looking like that. How humiliating!

When we finally made it to the side door of the castle, I was beyond relieved. All I could think about was taking that horrid ruffled hat off. And I did — the moment I stepped outside.

Erick lifted his hood to stare at me. "Timmy, what are you doing?"

"I'm becoming a boy again. Don't think I don't know that you two dressed me up like a girl!"

"Chambermaid," Gavril said. "And put the cap back on before someone recognizes you."

"Who's going to recognize me out here?"

Gavril gestured toward the front lawn of the castle. "They will."

I turned to look and was shocked to see the front lawn was teeming with people. It was hard to tell because it was still kind of dark, but I would be willing to swear some of them were having a picnic.

"What are they doing there?"

"They came to see you get exchanged for the mirror," Erick said.

"Really?" I looked again.

All those people came out at the crack of dawn to see something like that?

"But it's barely morning!" I said. "Don't they have anything better to do? Like sleep?"

Erick laughed. "Sure, but nothing is as entertaining as this."

I shook my head. "Man, they need cable TV here."

"We *need* to move on," Gavril said, looking agitated. "Let's go!"

Staying in the shadows, we skirted the castle until we reached the gardens in the back. Then we flitted as silently as ghosts from bush to bush, hoping to avoid anyone seeing us from one of the many castle windows.

I noticed that Gavril avoided the maze this time, which was perfectly fine with me. Frankly, I'm going to need years of therapy before I can ever set foot in a hedge maze again.

Gavril stopped us when we reached the edge of the gardens. A large field spread out before us, glowing gold in the rising sun. On the far side of the field was a thick strand of trees.

"The others are waiting for us in an old tower in the forest," Gavril said, pointing at the trees.

I looked. Sure enough, I could see the top of a tower poking out above the treetops.

"Cool! What's it used for?"

Gavril looked a bit startled, as though I had interrupted his train of thought. "It used to be an outlying defense for the castle."

"Way cool."

Gavril put his hand on my shoulder. "Now Tim, I need you to focus. We will be very visible crossing this field, so you must move fast. Do you understand?"

"You want me to run. Sure, I understand. I'm not a baby."

"I didn't say you were." Gavril glanced over his shoulder toward the castle and looked back at me. "Okay, run!"

I ran.

Of course, Erick and Gavril passed me within two seconds, but their legs were longer than mine.

And I really wasn't trying hard, anyway. It wasn't like we were being chased or anything.

We were about two thirds of the way across the field when I discovered I was wrong. Kat came bursting out from the woods like her hair was on fire. It wasn't really, but you'd *think* it was with the way she was acting.

"Hurry!" she cried, running toward us. "The soldiers are coming!"

"What? Where?" Gavril skidded to a stop and looked over his shoulder.

I looked back across the field, too. No soldiers.

It finally happened. Kat had lost her mind.

"I don't see anythi—" Gavril started to say.

"You can't from here," Kat said. "Ron saw them from the top of the tower. They were entering the gardens and coming this way."

Gavril sighed. "Great. I was hoping we would have more of a head start."

Me too.

We flew across the remainder of the field and plowed into the forest. Just a minute or so of scrambling through the underbrush brought us to the tall, somewhat-crumbling, stone tower.

Beriman was sitting on a fallen tree nearby, the mirror propped up next to him. He leapt to his feet when he saw me, and a big grin parted his bushy beard.

"Young Tim! You're alive!"

And then he gave me a hug that squeezed all the breath out of me.

"Beriman," Gavril said, glancing around the clearing. "Where is Ron?"

Beriman released me, and I gulped in some air

while he pointed up. "He's in the top of the tower."

Gavril bolted through the doorway. "Ron, get down here now!"

I peeked inside. The tower was empty, which wasn't surprising considering that a stone, spiral staircase took up much of the space. I looked up to see a wooden floor or platform at the top.

"Coming!" Ron called as his feet appeared at the top of the stairs.

Kat came up behind me. "Nice dress, Timmy."

I yanked off the frilly cap and threw it at her. "What? No 'Hi, Timmy, glad you're safe'? Some sister you are."

Wriggling out of the tunic, I balled it up, intending to toss it at her as well. But the look on her face stopped me.

"Sorry, Timmy," she said. "I really was worried. I'm glad you're okay."

Wait a minute... Did Kat just say she was sorry — to me? A Kat apology was about as rare as a Bigfoot sighting in downtown Miami.

All I could do is stand there and stare at her — with my mouth hanging open. Unfortunately, Gavril was paying more attention to Ron coming down the stairs than he was to us, so he missed the big moment.

"What's taking him so long?" he muttered, tossing aside his soldier's cloak. He next attempted to remove his chain mail — and got stuck.

"Tim, I could use a hand."

I grabbed ahold of the armor and helped hoist it over his head, but it was heavier than I expected. The moment it was clear of Gavril, it slipped from my fingers and landed on the floor with a thunk.

Gavril didn't seem to notice. He whisked off the rest of his disguise, looked up to check on Ron's progress, and let out a groan of what sounded like pure frustration.

I glanced up.

Despite the fact that soldiers were bearing down on us, Ron was picking his way down the stairs with those big feet of his as slowly as a sloth on vacation.

"Where did you last see the soldiers?" Gavril called up to him.

Ron paused to answer. "They were in the gardens. They're headed right this way."

"Then you'd better hurry."

"I *am* hurrying."

At that point, impatience was practically oozing out of Gavril's pores. He whipped around to face me and said: "Tim, go tell the others to be ready to leave the moment Ron gets down the stairs."

"Got it."

"And it better be soon," I heard Gavril mutter to himself as I rushed out the door.

Wizard Tim to the Rescue Again

"**H**urry, hurry!"

Gavril crashed through the underbrush with the mirror, thrusting aside any branch or twig that dared to get in his way.

Unfortunately, that just sent them swinging back at the next person in line.

Me.

After taking a couple of leafy smacks to the face, I let Kat get in front of me.

No, I wasn't being mean. I had just remembered my manners. Ladies first, you know.

"Where are we going, anyway?" Ron asked from somewhere behind me.

"Back to Castle Fenimore to destroy the mirror," said Gavril.

From the tone of his voice, I was quite sure Gavril was also thinking "Duh!" and rolling his eyes. I mean, where else would we be going?

Disneyland?

Of course, Ron, being Ron, didn't pick up on it.

"Wouldn't it be easier to take the road?"

Gavril gave a little snort and kept charging ahead like a bull toward a red cape. "Sure, but that would also make it easier for the queen's soldiers to catch us on horseback. Besides, cutting through the woods will take us right up into the hills."

A shortcut? Yep, that would be good. I couldn't see the soldiers yet when I looked back through the trees, but I could hear the commanders barking orders in the distance.

They weren't that far behind us.

Eventually, Gavril traded the underbrush for an actual trail, which made the going much easier.

Until we reached the hills, that is.

It wasn't long before my heart was pounding and my lungs were practically bursting. With all the hiking I had been doing since I went through Uncle Edgar's mirror, you'd think it would get easier for me.

But no such luck. The harder I tried, the farther Gavril seemed to pull ahead of us.

It was humiliating.

Ron, on the other hand, seemed to be thriving with all of our physical activity. He breezed by me and Kat on the trail and had the nerve to do it while whistling.

"Jerk," Kat muttered, leaning against a tree and breathing hard.

I found myself agreeing with her, but I didn't have the breath to tell her so. Too bad. That would have been a rare moment for us.

Beriman stopped behind us, panting. "This is ridiculous. We're never going to catch up with them. And the queen's soldiers are going to capture us and kill us."

Okay, *someone* was feeling grumpy.

Kat pushed back her damp hair. "Whatever, Beriman. I need a break."

"Me too," Erick puffed. "But we don't want to get too far behind the others." He cupped his hands around his mouth. "Gavril, wait up!"

Through the trees up ahead, I could see Gavril turn and motion to Ron to stop.

Erick took the lead. "Come on, everyone. We'll rest when we reach the others."

With a groan, I followed him to the relatively level spot where Gavril and Ron were standing and plopped down in the cool shade.

I needed a moment to catch my breath, so I was seriously annoyed when Gavril started poking me with his foot.

"Get up, Tim. We need to keep moving."

"Erick said we could rest."

"No time for that." Gavril pointed down the trail with his chin. "Take a look."

With a sigh, I pushed myself to my feet and looked where Gavril told me to. Through a break in the trees, I could see the castle below us. Otherwise, there were just a bunch of leaves and a few birds fluttering in the treetops.

And then my eyes caught some movement.

"Soldiers!"

I could only catch the glint of a helmet here and there through the leaves, but there was no doubt that an army of soldiers was making its way up the trail.

For a moment, I was impressed. They were making good time. But then I came to my senses and did what any normal human being in my situation would do.

I panicked. "Let's get out of here!"

Gavril, surprisingly, didn't budge. He seemed to be deep in thought.

"We're obviously not going to be able to outrun them."

Kat's face flushed. "We're moving as fast as we can, Gavril."

Gavril shot her a look. "Yes, I realize that. But the queen's men are in top condition. They will overtake us eventually."

Beriman plopped down on a fallen tree with a huff. "So what are we going to do? Just sit here and let them kill us?"

"No," Gavril said. "We outsmart them."

Ron frowned. "How?"

"Follow me."

Gavril took off running down the trail, heading straight for Mount Kern which was looming up in the distance.

I followed him more easily this time because the path was much more level. Besides, it's amazing how fast you can go when you know an army of soldiers is on your tail.

Of course, we couldn't keep up that pace forever. Gavril eventually slowed to a fast walk and even allowed us a few short breaks.

During one of those breaks, he asked a very odd question: "Beriman, do you know the tunnels under Mount Kern?"

Beriman scoffed. "I'm a dwarf. Of course I know those tunnels."

"How well do you know them?"

Beriman stared up at the mountain. "I worked in the silver mine for years, as did my father before me. It connects with those tunnels, you know. I remember playing in them as a child."

"What are you people talking about?" I asked,

looking up from my video game. (Yep, I was playing my video game again. It helps me relax.)

Gavril sat down next to me in the grass. "Many years ago, the dwarves dug an intricate network of tunnels under the mountain."

"There are natural caves, too," Beriman said. "The tunnels connect them."

Erick nodded. "That's right. I had forgotten all about that. If we could use those tunnels, it would cut hours off our journey."

Gavril nodded. "Exactly. I think it's our only hope of getting to the castle before the soldiers catch up to us."

Beriman looked unsure. "But it's been years since I've been in those tunnels. I don't know if I can remember the way. And what about Akar?"

"Who's Akar?" I asked.

"No one you need to worry about, Tim," Gavril said, getting to his feet. "Come on. We have no time to waste."

I shoved my video game into my pocket and scrambled after him. We spent the next couple of hours on the trail, trying to keep up with Energizer Bunny Gavril and trying to stay in front of the soldiers.

Eventually, Gavril crouched down behind some bushes and motioned for the rest of us to do the same. Parting some branches, I looked across a clearing to see a large hole cut into the mountain.

The mine. And, apparently, our entrance to the tunnels under the mountain.

Like the other mine we had encountered on our journey, this one was guarded by a couple of soldiers. One of them had red hair and freckles, and the other had a squashed-in nose like a bulldog.

They both looked bored.

Gavril motioned us all closer so he could speak in a whisper. "We need to deal with the guards. Kat, you stay here with the mirror."

Kat took it from him reluctantly. "Are you sticking me with the mirror because I'm a girl? I can fight, you know."

"Yes, I know. But I need you here."

"You don't have a weapon anyway," I whispered. "Remember? The guards took your bow and arrows away in the dungeon."

"I could borrow Ron's sword," she whispered back fiercely.

Gavril shook his head. "Kat, you're staying here."

Kat gave a little huff. "Fine."

"Now, Ron and I are the only ones with swords," Gavril said, ignoring Kat's obviously stinky attitude. "So I need someone to distract the soldiers while the two of us sneak up behind them. Any volunteers?"

I leapt to my feet. "I'll do it!"

And then I plunged through the bushes into the clearing before he could say no.

"Timmy, get back here," Kat hissed. "You'll get yourself killed!"

Why was she always saying that? Had she already forgotten how Wizard Tim and his "little magic box" saved the day in the dungeon? Pulling my game out of my pocket, I powered it up and turned the sound back on.

When I glanced up, I noticed the soldiers were looking a lot less bored. They had spotted me and were already moving in my direction.

Game on!

"What have we here?" Mr. Freckles asked.

I pointed my game at them. "I'm a great wizard. If you don't do exactly as I say, I'll shrink you down to the size of a fly and make you my prisoners in this little box. Forever!"

The men stared at me with their mouths hanging open. And then they started to laugh. And laugh. And laugh.

They laughed so hard that they were doubled over.

Not exactly the response I was hoping for.

"You're going to take us prisoner?" Mr. Bulldog asked when he could finally speak. "In that little box?"

"Yeah, so you'd better not take another step closer, or you'll be sorry."

The two soldiers looked at each other, smiled, and took a step forward.

"I'm warning you!" I stepped back, fighting to keep my hand steady. "I'm not afraid to use this!"

The soldiers drew their swords and took two more very deliberate steps.

I began to break out in a sweat.

Where were Ron and Gavril?

And then I saw them. They had worked their way around the clearing and were stepping out from the bushes behind the soldiers.

My confidence soared.

"Okay, have it your way," I said to the soldiers. "Prepare to be shrunk."

With my best evil villain laugh, I pushed a button on my game. Ominous-sounding music began to play.

The soldiers leapt back, their swords raised and their eyes wide. They stared at the video game in my hand, oblivious to everything else.

And that's when Gavril and Ron made their move. They stepped up and pressed the tips of their swords to the soldiers' backs.

"Drop your weapons," Gavril said.

The soldiers wisely did as they were told.

I swept their swords up from the ground and proudly slipped one of them into my empty sheath. "Not bad, huh?"

"You idiot," Ron said from behind the red-haired soldier. "You really lucked out this time. These guys could have cut you into little pieces."

"That was the plan," Freckles muttered.

"See?" Ron said.

I shook my head. "No way. I had them right where I wanted the whole time."

"Sure you did, Timmy," Kat said as she stepped through the bushes with Beriman and Erick.

"It's Tim," I reminded her. "And you're just jealous because you were stuck holding the mirror while I was busy saving the day."

"You're crazy."

"Like a fox!" I waved the spare sword. "And look what I've got for you, Erick!"

Erick took it from me with a grin. "Thanks, Timmy. Uh, I mean, Tim."

"Okay, men," Gavril said, still tickling Pug Nose's back with his sword. "Start walking toward the entrance of the mine. Slowly."

The soldiers looked unhappy about it, but they obeyed.

When they started to move forward, Gavril turned his attention to the rest of us.

"Stay close behind us and be ready for anything."

Anything?

I drew my sword and gripped it tightly as we entered the mine. At first, I couldn't see a thing. It took a few moments for my eyes to adjust after coming in from the bright sunshine outside.

And then I peeked around the soldiers we had captured... and wow!

Flickering torches hung on the walls, lighting up a large space carved out of stone. Dwarves were rushing here and there, making the place look as busy as Grand Central Station during rush hour. Some were carrying pickaxes into the tunnels. Others were hauling heavy-looking buckets of rocks out of the tunnels.

They all looked miserable, and I soon saw why.

A couple dozen soldiers were standing guard, occasionally barking orders and shoving around the dwarves who weren't obeying them fast enough.

"More soldiers?" Kat whispered, hugging the mirror to her chest. "It would have been nice to know about them before we waltzed in here."

Gavril shushed her and nudged our captives forward. And it took all of two seconds for a particularly mean-looking soldier with a short goatee to spot them.

"What are you two doing in here? You are supposed to be on guard outside." Then he noticed the rest of us and whipped out his sword.

"Intruders!"

And that got the attention of the other soldiers.

A ringing sound filled the mine as swords were drawn from sheaves.

I was really beginning to hate that noise.

Beriman didn't seem to be intimidated in the least. He stepped out in front of the soldiers, his beard bristling.

"Your queen is defeated!" he cried. "Lay down your weapons and surrender to us now!"

Yeah, he was exaggerating a little.

Okay, a lot. But I had to admire his chutzpah, as my grandpa used to say.

The soldiers seemed a bit surprised. They looked at Beriman. They looked at the rest of us.

And then they all began to laugh.

Yeah, I got laughed at twice in one day. It was worse than middle school.

The soldier with the goatee raised his hand and the laughter died instantly. The silence was almost deafening.

After several long moments, Goatee Guy pointed his bony finger at us and said two simple words:

"Kill them!"

Revenge of the Dwarves

Kill them?

Really?

Was that *all* they taught these guys in Soldier School? Whatever happened to that whole "you're innocent until proven guilty" thing? They really ought to try *that* sometime.

Anyway, there must have been some kind of expression on my face — like, I don't know, complete terror — because Beriman was quick to say:

"Fear not, Tim. We've got them outnumbered."

Outnumbered? By my count, *we* were the ones outnumbered — four to one. Beriman was even worse at math than Ron was!

But Beriman seemed to have a plan.

He raised his hand to get everyone's attention and cried out in a loud voice: "My people, listen to me! The queen no longer has any power over you. We have captured her evil mirror!"

He then grabbed the mirror from a surprised Kat, tore off its velvet covering, and held it high over his head.

"Look!"

It glittered and sparkled in his hands in the dim light of the mine, drawing gasps of awe from the dwarves and a gasp of horror from Gavril. "Beriman, cover up the mirror! Have you gone mad?"

Beriman opened his mouth to answer, but that was as far as he got.

A battle cry filled the mine. It bounced off the rock walls, echoing louder and louder until it sounded like it was being made by thousands of men.

The soldiers were attacking!

I whirled around to face what I was sure was certain doom — and was shocked to see the queen's men scattering like cockroaches when you turn the light on.

Huh? I blinked to make sure I was seeing straight.

I was!

The dwarves had turned on their captors with a sudden fierceness, swinging their pickaxes, throwing rocks, and flinging their pails at any unlucky soldier within their reach.

It was like watching a pack of really ticked-off Chihuahuas attack a bunch of Dobermans. A few of the guards stood their ground and fought back. But most of them — including the two we had captured outside — made a mad dash for the exit like a bunch of lily-livered wimps.

It was awesome!

In fact, it was so entertaining, I could have watched it all day. But Gavril had other plans for us.

"Everyone, grab some torches," he said, pointing to a pile of what looked like sticks with rags wrapped around one end. "We're going to need light when we reach the tunnels."

We quickly obeyed, snatching up as many torches as we could and sorting them into two bundles to add to our packs.

When we were done, Ron and Erick strapped the awkward, top-heavy packs onto their backs as best they could. And Gavril took the mirror — once again wrapped in its velvet cloth — from Beriman.

"Let's get moving," he said. "Beriman, lead on."

Beriman gave a quick nod and started off, easing around the fighting and rounding a corner to head deeper into the mine.

We immediately encountered a large group of dwarves herding some unhappy-looking soldiers toward the entrance. One look at their fierce expressions, and I pitied the soldiers.

Well, almost.

Beriman gave a chuckle. "I wish I had known the guards were such a bunch of cowards. I'd have caused a riot years ago."

"And gotten yourself killed, most likely," Gavril said.

"Don't judge me by my size, my good prince. I can out-fight most any man. Maybe even you!"

Gavril stopped and gave him a low bow. "I'm sure you can. I stand corrected, my friend."

Conversation dwindled away as we went deeper into the mine. My guess is that no one felt like talking much. I know I sure didn't. Despite the valiant efforts of the torches hanging on the walls, it was dark, damp, chilly, and kind of depressing.

Only Beriman seemed cheerful. You'd think he was on holiday or something. I swear I heard him humming to himself as he led us down one passageway after another. For hours.

We didn't stop until we reached a hole.

A big one.

"It's a mine shaft," Beriman said. "It goes deep into the earth."

"Let me see."

I walked cautiously to the edge and looked down. Yep, it was deep all right. I could see tiny torches way down below, flickering like miniature fireflies.

Tour Guide Beriman clapped his hands to get our attention. "Everyone, come this way. We'll be following this shaft for some distance until we arrive at the great stone bridge that spans it. Please take care not to fall in."

Kat looked at me. "He means *you*, Timmy."

"No, he means *you*."

"I'm not the klutz. You are."

"Am not!"

"Are too!"

"Give it a rest, you two," Erick said. "You're not five-year-olds."

Kat sniffed. "Well, Timmy acts like one."

"I do not!"

"Enough!" Gavril shouted from somewhere behind us.

The mine echoed back: Enough... enough... enough... enough... enough... enough... enough... enough...

The effect was so cool that I forgot all about arguing with Kat, at least for the moment. That allowed me to pay more attention to my surroundings, which was probably a good thing.

Walking alongside the "one-wrong-step-and-you're-dead" shaft was more nerve-wracking than I cared to admit. I stayed as close to the wall as possible.

I'm no dummy.

Eventually, Beriman resumed his tour guide act, gesturing toward a crumbling structure that spanned the crevice.

"Here is the great stone bridge. It was engineered by dwarves hundreds of years ago and is a stunning example of my people's handiwork."

I was stunned all right. The so-called bridge was only about two feet wide, and it had no hand rails to keep me from plummeting thousands of feet to my death.

My mom would lose her mind if she saw it.

Plus, there were a bunch of gaping holes where rocks were supposed to be — but weren't. Would it even hold us? Or would it come tumbling down like a Jenga game?

Kat pointed at the bridge, her eyes huge. "We're supposed to cross *that*?"

"Beriman, are you sure there isn't another way?" Gavril asked.

Beriman shook his head. "This is the only way into the tunnels. And the caves."

Silence. I could hear a stone fall into the shaft — and I swear it came from that sorry-excuse-for-a-bridge.

"But Gavril," Kat said, "we can't go over that thing! It's not safe!"

Understatement of the year.

Gavril shrugged. "I'm sorry, Kat, but we have no choice."

Kat continued to sputter away, but no understandable words were coming out of her mouth. So Gavril chose to ignore her and turned to the rest of us.

"We'll need some light."

Erick yanked off his pack and fumbled with the rope around it. "How many torches do you want to use?"

"Just three. We'll space them out as we cross so everyone can see where they're going."

Erick handed a torch to both Gavril and Beriman, keeping one for himself.

"Hey, don't I get one?" I asked.

Erick shook his head as he lit his torch. "Sorry, Tim. I'd much rather you have both hands free when you cross the bridge. As it is, your mother is going to kill me if she finds out I let you set foot on a structure like that."

"I still don't like it," Kat said.

Gavril got his torch lit. "Everyone ready?"

Silence again, which apparently Gavril took as a big "yes." He wasted no time in continuing.

"Then we'll proceed in single file. Beriman, you go first. I'll take up the rear. And everyone, please move carefully. This thing doesn't look very sturdy."

I stand corrected. *That* was the understatement of the year.

Holding his flaming torch high — which isn't saying much, considering how short he is — Beriman stepped out onto the bridge.

"I don't know what you people are complaining about," he said. "This bridge is perfectly safe. It's as sturdy as an old boot."

As sturdy as an old boot? Yeah, that made me feel so much better.

I stepped to the side and let Ron go next. He was

followed by Kat, who was still muttering something under her breath, and then Erick.

It was my turn. I could feel my palms sweating and my legs shaking as I walked out onto the bridge that crossed the "Crater of Doom."

Yeah, I gave the shaft a name. Believe me, it totally fits.

All I did was take one look at the darkness beyond my feet and the sweat on my palms immediately shot all the way up to my armpits.

It was *that* scary. It reminded me of a scene in one of my favorite movies where the characters also had to cross a sorry-looking stone bridge that had been built by dwarves.

Yeah, dwarves. Just like this one.

Coincidence? I doubted it.

But if this bridge started to fall apart in chunks like that one did, I was going to pee my pants. Or die. Or both.

Then a strange sound startled me out of my thoughts.

Was that thunder?

Kat stopped and looked around. "What was that noise?"

"Everyone, keep going," Gavril said from behind me. "We need to get off this bridge now."

"Why?" I asked. "What's going on?"

"Just move, Tim!"

Before I had a chance to even take one step, something dark and huge flew over us and let out an ear-splitting roar that shook the entire bridge.

Kat screamed, and we all hit the deck, so to speak. As I clung to the trembling bridge, I could hear a shower of stones falling into the cavern below.

Okay, that definitely wasn't thunder.

"What was that?" Ron yelled.

"Akar!" Beriman yelled back.

"What's an Akar?" I asked.

There was another roar, and we all ducked our heads as the shadow swooped over us again. A stream of flames burst from its mouth, lighting up the entire cavern and answering my question.

Akar was a dragon.

How to Outrun a Dragon

"Everyone on your feet!" Gavril said. "Run!"

He didn't have to tell us twice. We scrambled up and ran like we were being chased by a fire-breathing dragon.

Which we WERE!

Was I worried any more about falling off that narrow, crumbling bridge? Nope. All I cared about at that moment was NOT being charbroiled to a crisp.

"It's coming back!" Kat screamed.

I glanced over my shoulder. The dragon, who was still spitting fire like crazy, had banked its wings and was making a wide turn.

"Faster!" Gavril yelled.

I gave a little moan. I couldn't go any faster over the uneven bridge unless I sprouted wings and flew. And we all know *that* wasn't likely to happen.

Up ahead, Beriman cleared the end of the bridge with a leap. "The tunnel entrance is here," he called. "We'll be safe once we're inside."

Great. One glance told me the dragon was bearing down on us like a fiery freight train. And I was only halfway across the bridge. There was no way I would make it to the tunnel in time.

I was toast.

Correction: I was *burnt* toast.

But at least my brother and sister would live to

tell the tale of how their baby brother got incinerated by a dragon.

In the light of Beriman's torch, I could see Ron clear the end of the bridge with a giant leap while dragging Kat with him. One look at the oncoming dragon sent them scurrying into the tunnel with Beriman like rabbits into a hole.

Just three of us left. And we were out of time.

The dragon gave a roar and swooped low. Erick, Gavril, and I flung ourselves down and hugged the bridge. I could feel the heat of the dragon's flames as it flew over us.

"Up!" Erick cried, yanking me to my feet as soon as the coast was clear.

"Hurry!" Gavril yelled. "It's coming back again!"

What? *Already?*

Trying to keep low, I scrambled after Erick. But I didn't get more than just a few steps before I had to flatten myself on the bridge again.

This time, I swear the dragon cranked the heat up a notch. Clouds of sulfurous smoke surrounded us, making me choke.

"I hate this!"

"I'm not loving it either, Timmy," Erick said. "Now come on."

He grabbed my arm and hauled me to the end of the bridge. Gavril was right on my heels. Unfortunately, so was the dragon.

We had just managed to duck into the tunnel when the creature belched out an inferno of flames that made its previous efforts seem downright wimpy.

Tongues of fire licked at our backs as we joined

the others and raced deeper into the passageway. I don't think I ever ran so fast in my life. I even passed by Ron.

As soon as we out-distanced the flames, Erick slowed his pace. "I think we're safe now."

We all stopped and looked at each other in the light of the three torches. For a long moment, no one said anything.

"Is everyone okay?" Gavril finally asked.

I shrugged. None of us appeared to be on fire, so I guess that was a plus. But apparently, Kat didn't see it that way.

"No, we're not okay," Kat said, her voice higher pitched than usual. "We almost got roasted alive by a dragon!"

"Akar," Beriman said.

I looked straight at Gavril. "Isn't that the Akar you told us not to worry about?"

But Kat was too fired up to give him a chance to answer. "It was a dragon, Gavril. A dragon! How could you not warn us about a fire-breathing dragon?"

Ron came up behind her. "Yeah!"

Yep, that's all we got from Ron, but it was said with great feeling.

Erick ran his hand over his beard and stepped back. "I'm staying out of this one."

Gavril's eyes flicked to him before coming back to us. "I'm sorry. I didn't know for sure that Akar was here."

"I didn't either," Beriman said. "I thought the dragon was just a rumor. A tall tale told to us by the guards to keep us from trying to escape through the tunnels."

"Well, obviously it wasn't a rumor," Kat said. "And even if that's all it was, you still should have said something. If I knew there was even a possibility of a dragon in these tunnels, I never would have agreed to come this way."

Gavril looked like he wanted to throw his hands up in exasperation, but he couldn't. He was too busy holding the mirror and a torch.

"Dragon or no dragon, we *had* to come this way!"

Kat looked furious enough to spit. "But we could have all been killed by that thing!"

"But we weren't killed. We got away from the dragon. We're safe."

Kat crossed her arms. "Sure, Gavril. But what if he comes after us, huh?"

"How? Akar can't fit into this tunnel."

Kat pursed her lips together and looked around. She must have seen that Gavril had a point. *We* could barely fit in the tunnel. Ron's head came just a few inches from the ceiling!

"Whatever," she muttered.

Gavril sighed. "Good. Now that we've got that cleared up, let's get moving."

Our journey through the tunnels had to be the most tedious, mind-numbing thing I've ever done.

Ever.

It was always dark. It was always cold. And there was no sense of time. We could walk for days, and I wouldn't know it.

And it was always boring.

Well, almost always. Occasionally, we came to a section of tunnel that was so narrow we had to squeeze through sideways. Beriman, who was a bit rounder than the rest of us, almost got stuck once. That was fun.

But most of the time, it was about as exciting as sitting in a classroom and listening to Mr. Burton, my science teacher, drone on and on about earthworms.

Eventually, after like two days, Gavril called a halt for the night. (Well, maybe it *wasn't* two days, but who could tell in that place?)

Kat sat down on the rocky floor with a huff.

Ron plopped down beside her. "What's wrong with you?"

I sat down next to him. "What's wrong with Kat? I've been waiting for someone to ask. I've got a list. She's bossy, stubborn, irritable, grouchy —"

"Timmy, enough!" Erick said, giving me his sternest look before turning to my sister. "Now, Kat, what's wrong?"

She shrugged. "Nothing. I'm just not thrilled to be spending a night in a cave, that's all."

"Tunnel," I said.

Kat glared at me. "Same thing!"

"I don't think any of us are looking forward to sleeping down here, Kat," Erick said.

Beriman snorted. "Speak for yourself. Dwarves love to be underground. Besides, it was my ancestors who built these tunnels. I feel quite at home."

"That makes one of us," Kat said, her voice breaking. "I wish I was back at Grandma's house."

I studied her in the flickering torchlight. "Me too," I said softly.

"Kat, just hang in there," Erick said, touching

her arm. "I'll do everything I can to get you all home soon."

Gavril leaned forward. "As will I. But right now, please try to get some rest. We have quite some distance to go to reach the other side of the mountain, and you'll need your strength."

Kat nodded and settled down against the wall. She seemed to relax a little, but I couldn't.

I simply couldn't take my eyes off our only lit torch.

It was propped up nearby with some rocks, which was fine. But, it was also giving off a lot of smoke which, I assumed, was *not* fine.

If that thing went out, we would be left in complete darkness. And there was no way I was going to sleep in a cave — I mean, tunnel — in the pitch dark.

No way.

I had to say something: "Uh, Gavril, I think the torch is going out."

Gavril opened one eye to look at it and then closed it again. "That's okay, Tim. You don't need light to sleep."

"Yeah, but if I hear a scary noise while I'm trying to sleep, I want to be able to see what's making it."

Ron sat up. "You know, Timmy has a point there. We don't really know what's in these tunnels with us, do we?"

"Exactly!" I said. "What if we're lying in the dark and hear something big walking through the tunnel toward us, growling and gnashing its teeth? What would we do?"

Gavril opened one eye again. "Light a torch."

"Yes, but suppose Ron can't find his matches. Or

even worse, he drops them. We'd be sitting ducks."

"I wouldn't drop the matches," Ron said.

"You might."

"So what happens next, Tim?" Beriman asked.

I looked at him, surprised. Apparently, dwarves like scary bedtime stories. Who knew?

With my most dramatic storytelling voice, I continued: "The creature would leap on us in the darkness. We wouldn't be able to fight back because we wouldn't be able to see it. So it would tear us all to pieces. The end."

Gavril got to his feet, laughing. "Okay, Tim! I'll light a fresh torch. Just go to sleep!"

Despite the torchlight, I didn't think I'd ever fall asleep in the tunnel. Not only was it cold and drafty, but the floor was as hard as a rock.

Literally.

But I must have drifted off at some point because, the next thing I knew, a hand was shaking me awake.

"Tim, get up."

I cracked my eyes, saw Gavril, and rolled over. "Give me a break. It's not morning yet. It's still dark."

"We're in a cave, stupid," Kat said. "What do you think it's going to be?"

She's always grumpy when she first wakes up, especially in caves. And tunnels.

And pretty much everywhere else.

After a quick and unsatisfying breakfast of deer jerky, we hit the road again, so to speak, guided by the still cheerful Beriman.

"Observe the different layers of color in the rock," he said, gesturing. "You can tell that water flowed through here at one time. An underground river, perhaps."

I frowned, thinking. "So are you saying that this tunnel was already here when the dwarves cut their way through the mountain?"

Beriman stopped and turned to face me. "Yes, it must have been. I remember my grandfather telling me stories of the beautiful caverns my people found down here."

"I wonder if the river is still here," Kat said. "Our water bottles could use some refilling."

"We're running out of water?" I asked.

"Don't worry, Timmy," Ron said. "We'll be out of these tunnels in no time, right, Beriman?"

Beriman's beard waggled as he shook his head. "No. We have some distance to go yet."

"But what about water?"

Gavril clapped a hand on my back. "Don't worry, Tim. We'll just ration what we have left until we find a water source."

A "water source" in the middle of a mountain? I wasn't holding my breath on that one.

I Strike It Rich

Hours later, I was still worrying about water.

What can I say? I was thirsty.

But then I noticed something that gave me hope.

"Hey, we're going uphill! We're almost out of here!"

"Not yet, Tim," Beriman said.

"No, really! We *must* be near the end. Don't you feel that breeze?" I lifted my face and spread out my arms so I could enjoy it better.

It really felt good.

"That draft could be coming from some natural caves," Gavril said. "Not the outside."

"I just hope it doesn't blow out the torch," Kat said.

As we walked on, the breeze grew stronger and stronger. Then, without warning, the walls and the ceiling sprang away from us. I suddenly felt a ton of empty space around me.

"Where are we?" I asked.

Gavril raised his torch. "It's a large cavern."

It was AMAZING!

Imagine the coolest, most awesome cave that Hollywood could dream up. Throw in a bunch of gigantic rock icicles hanging down, some grand stone pillars, and a rock formation that looked like a flowing waterfall. And that would give you a bit of an idea of what I was seeing.

Ron gave a low whistle. "Wow! We need more light."

For once, Gavril didn't argue. "Get another torch."

Ron did. The extra light made a huge difference. We walked around for a few minutes, taking everything in.

"Hey, Kat," I said. "Check out that pointy rock coming out of the floor. It looks like a skinny Empire State building, doesn't it?"

"That's not a pointy rock, Timmy. It's a stalagmite."

"Oh, and I suppose you have a fancy name for the stone icicles coming off the ceiling, too."

"They're stalactites."

I looked at her. "You're no fun, you know that?"

Kat shrugged. "If you paid attention in school, you might know this stuff, Timmy."

I was tempted to stick my tongue out at her. (Yeah, I know. Real mature.) But I was distracted by some strange, sniffling noises that were coming from Beriman.

Was he *crying*?

"Are you okay, Beriman?"

Beriman wiped his eyes with the back of his hand.

He *was* crying!

"I haven't been in this cavern since I was very young," he said with another sniffle. "I had forgotten how beautiful it is."

I shifted uncomfortably. What's a guy supposed to do when another guy (or dwarf) cries? Talk about awkward. Fortunately, Gavril came to my rescue.

"Everyone! Over here!" he called.

I scrambled over to him as fast as I could. "Did you find treasure?"

Seriously, a chest of pirate doubloons was all the cave needed to be ultra-cool.

"No, something better." Gavril pointed down. "Look."

Water! I dropped to my knees by a small stream that was flowing out of a crevice in the wall.

"We're saved!"

We all took a good, long drink before filling up the water skins. Then we broke out the deer jerky for a little snack right there by the underground stream.

It was like a picnic, but without the sandwiches or the ants.

Gavril finally stood up and tucked the mirror in its usual place under his arm. "We need to get moving."

I looked around. "Which way do we go?"

There were several black holes in the walls of the cavern. Some were tall and wide, and others were short and narrow. But all of them looked like tunnels.

Beriman stood still, sniffing the air.

Yeah, you read that right. He was sniffing the air like a dog smelling a pizza.

Weird. But if that's what he had to do to get us out of there, I wasn't about to criticize.

"We go this way," Beriman finally said, heading toward the opposite end of the cavern.

I followed behind him eagerly enough at first — until something shiny caught my eye.

"Hey, what is that?" I asked, pointing.

"Maybe it's some kind of quartz," Kat said. "That can sparkle, can't it?"

Gavril frowned. "Not like that."

I started to get excited. "Maybe we've discovered gold. We'll be rich!"

"Take it easy, Tim," Erick said. "Things aren't always what they appear to be."

Beriman started to walk faster. "Look at the way it's reflecting the light, Tim. It very well could be gold!"

As we drew closer, it seemed that whatever was making the sparkle was in a nook in the side of the cavern. Beriman hurried toward it, and I was right on his heels.

"You two had better not get your hopes up," Kat said, trailing behind us. "The chances of us finding gold down here are—"

"Whoo-hoo!"

That was me. I was whooping and hollering and doing the happy dance arm-in-arm with Beriman.

And Kat just stood there with her mouth hanging open.

The nook was full of treasure.

Treasure!

Gold coins lay in large, glittering heaps on the stone floor. Large precious gems — such as diamonds, rubies, and emeralds — were scattered carelessly about as if they were just regular stones. And ancient wooden chests were overflowing with ropes of pearls and other fancy jewelry.

There were even some weapons — including jewel-studded swords and shields — piled up in one corner.

"We're rich!" I abandoned my happy dance and dove right into the middle of the piles of gold, scattering coins everywhere.

Beriman handed his torch to Kat and jumped in beside me. Ron immediately followed. While my brother and I scooped up handfuls of coins and tossed them in the air (like the millionaires on TV do), Beriman shuffled over to the pile of weapons and pounced upon a short jewel-studded sword.

"This was made by dwarves," he said, thrusting it through his belt with a satisfied grunt. "It'll do just fine. Oh, yes. Just fine."

And then he got busy stuffing as much gold as possible into his tunic.

Strangely, Kat, Erick, and Gavril didn't join in the fun. They just stood there watching us from the entrance of the nook. Gavril actually looked nervous, glancing over his shoulder at times into the darkness of the cavern behind him.

"What is all this stuff?" I asked, letting a handful of coins run through my fingers. "Pirates' loot?"

"No," Gavril said. "I think we've stumbled into the dragon's lair."

"Dragon?" Kat's eyes got huge. "Not Akar!"

"It had better be Akar," Erick said. "I would hate to think we're dealing with a second dragon."

Kat was shaking her head. "No, it can't be. Gavril said Akar couldn't fit into the tunnel."

"There are many passageways in this mountain that Akar can use," Gavril said. "And look around. This cavern is plenty big for a dragon. It's big enough for a hundred dragons."

Kat's eyes got even larger, if that was possible. "Then we need to get out of here!"

"Not without some of this treasure, we don't!" I said.

I dumped the jewelry out of one of the small

wooden chests and started filling it with handfuls of coins.

Kat gasped. "Timmy, we don't have time for that!"

I paused and looked straight at her. "Kat, we lost our home, and Mom is working two jobs. We need this."

Erick looked shocked. "You lost your home, and Elaine is working two jobs? How did that happen?"

"Mom didn't earn enough money with her grocery store job to make the rent payments on the house after you disappeared," Kat said. "She started cleaning houses, too, but it still wasn't enough."

"Yeah," Ron said, glancing up from shoving coins into his pockets. "That's why we had to move in with Grandma and creepy Uncle Edgar."

Erick ran his hand through his hair. "Poor Elaine. I need to get back there. *We* need to get back there."

Gavril glanced over his shoulder into the dark cavern again. "I would like nothing better than to send you *all* back there. But we need to get out of here first. Now!"

I stood up, hauling the chest with me. Although it was small, it was heavier than I expected. But that didn't matter. I was going to carry it home with me if I had to tie a rope around it and drag it the entire way.

Actually, that wasn't such a bad idea.

"Anyone see a rope?"

My question was answered by a loud scraping noise in the cavern. It sounded like something huge was moving along the rocky floor.

My heart flipped like an acrobat as Gavril and

Kat whirled to face the noise with their torches. I scrambled to stand beside them, clutching the box of coins to my chest.

"I can't see anything," I whispered, wishing the torches threw more light. "Is it the dragon?"

I was answered by a loud roar and a burst of flames that lit up the amazing rock formations of the cavern like a fireworks display.

Uh, that would be a big YES.

Gavril shoved the mirror into Ron's arms and whipped out his sword. "Beriman, get us out of here!"

The dragon roared again and lurched forward, belching out fire like a blowtorch on steroids. Its giant wings seemed to fill the cavern, and its long tail sent large rocks scattering across the floor. The scales of its skin glinted like armor in the light.

It was terrifying. We froze like a herd of deer on a busy highway. Well, all of us except for Gavril, that is. Dragons must be old news to him.

"Beriman, go!" Gavril said. "Lead us!"

"This way!" Beriman cried, grabbing his torch back from Kat and bolting toward the end of the cavern.

Coins burst from his bulging tunic like popcorn as he ran, which looked really funny.

But no one laughed.

Seriously, would you feel like laughing if a ticked-off dragon was standing within flame-throwing distance from you? I sure didn't.

Besides, Akar picked that exact moment to launch off with its enormous feet and soar over our heads. Just one look at its scaled belly told me what I already suspected.

We were goners.

How were we supposed to fight a creature covered head-to-toe in armor with only our swords? At the very least, we needed a rocket launcher.

The dragon expertly twisted its body in mid-air, landed with an earth-shaking thud in front of us, and spouted off another volley of flames.

"Get back!" Gavril hollered. "Get back!"

My sneakers skidded on some loose rocks as I tried to reverse my direction mid-run. My feet went one way, my body went another, and my precious chest of coins flew from my hands.

"Nooooo!" I cried as I watched the box hit the rocky floor and burst open. Gold coins spilled out in a bright, glittering heap.

I scrambled up from where I had landed hard on my butt, and I lunged for the coins.

Only to be yanked back by Gavril.

"Stay back!" he yelled. "Are you crazy?"

Akar bellowed out a firestorm, incinerating what was left of the box, and sending us fleeing for shelter behind the rocks.

Smoke filled the air, making me cough. Shaking, I huddled behind one of Kat's stalagmites and peeked out.

At first, the smoke was too thick for me to see a thing. But the drafts of the cavern worked quickly to break it up and whisk it away, making the dragon as easy to spot as a skyscraper in a desert.

It was standing over the pile of spilled coins.

And looking right at me.

I ducked lower behind the rock.

Maybe it would stop staring if it couldn't see me.

I snuck another peek.

Nope. Still staring.

"Thief!"

I jumped at the sound of the deep, raspy voice. Who on earth was that?

Peering around the rock again, I saw that the dragon had slithered closer. And its gaze was still on me.

"No one takes my gold, little thief."

Horrified, I ducked back behind the stalagmite. I couldn't believe my eyes or my ears.

The dragon was *talking*.

To me!

I sat there for several seconds, my mind in a tailspin.

Think! Think!

How did Bilbo Baggins handle the talking dragon in *The Hobbit*? I couldn't remember. My brain just kept spinning uselessly like a car engine stuck in neutral.

In a panic, I looked at the others. But they weren't paying attention to me. They were all staring wide-eyed at something above me.

With a sinking feeling, I looked up — right into the black, beady eyes of the dragon.

Never Steal from a Dragon

"**A**RGHHHHH!"

Yes, that was me. Yelling.

Akar's head was so close that I could reach up and touch it.

But I didn't.

I'm not *that* crazy. I pushed off my butt and scurried away from the dragon on my hands and feet in the fastest crab walk ever.

And slammed right into Gavril.

"Gavril, help!" I squeaked.

Gavril stepped in front of me, his sword raised. "You've got your gold, Akar. Let us pass in peace."

The dragon studied us, wisps of smoke curling up from its nostrils. "Not so fast, little prince."

"You know who I am?"

"Yes, Gavril of Tryton," Akar said. "I know your name. And I know that three of your number have touched my gold."

It was at that moment a gold coin slipped from Ron's overflowing pockets and clattered onto the rocky floor.

Worst. Timing. Ever.

Akar stared at him and gave a low growl.

Looking panicked, Ron shoved the mirror into Kat's hands and emptied his pockets onto the cave floor. "Here's your gold, Mr. Dragon. See? You can have it all back."

The dragon's eyes narrowed, and flames of fire mixed with the smoke started coming from its nose.

"Everyone take cover," Gavril yelled. "Now!"

We dove behind the rocks just as a burst of fire shot forth from Akar's mouth. Smoke billowed around us again. But that time, it worked in our favor.

"Beriman, get everyone out of here, now," Gavril said, "and wait for me at the first bend in the tunnel."

He didn't have to tell Beriman twice. He took off running into the dark mist with the rest of us following as close as a shadow.

Akar must have sensed that we were trying to slip away. It roared out another firestorm and poured more smoke into the cavern.

At first I was thrilled. The dragon really couldn't see us now! Ha, ha! The joke was on Akar!

But then I realized I couldn't see much of anything either.

The joke was on me.

I quickly lost sight of the others except for the glimmer of a torch somewhere ahead of me. I stretched out my hands, ran blindly in that direction, and almost immediately fell hard over a rock.

"Ow!"

I grabbed at my aching knee, but I couldn't see how badly I hurt it.

Actually, I couldn't see anything. The torch had vanished. Everyone had run off and left me alone in the dark with a sore knee and a dragon I couldn't see!

I was about to start a little pity party for myself

right then and there, but it was at that moment I noticed a warm glow breaking through the dark and smoke clouds ahead of me.

A torch! I wasn't abandoned in the darkness. Someone was looking for me!

Wincing a little at the pain in my knee, I stumbled to my feet. "Over here!"

The torch drew nearer. With the smoke still fairly heavy around me, it was hard to see who was carrying it. But I didn't care. Help was coming. That was what was important.

Suddenly, the smoky clouds parted like curtains on a stage. And my blood froze.

That was no torch.

It was the dragon!

What I thought was the torch was actually a low, simmering fire that was coming out of the dragon's mouth.

Great. I didn't think it could be possible, but my day just got worse.

Akar smiled, revealing two rows of long, razor-sharp teeth. "Well, well, well. It's the little thief. Just the one I was looking for."

I swallowed hard and backed up a step.

The dragon glided forward, its long tail twisting on the floor like a snake. "No one takes my gold and lives to tell about it, little thief."

Then it lowered its immense head and looked at me eye-to-eye. "No one."

I stood frozen in place, my mind racing. The smoke had disappeared, so I couldn't hide in it. And I wouldn't have a chance of making it to a tunnel without some light.

There was no way to escape. I was officially

dead meat.

I was beyond scared. I was beyond thinking. So I did the craziest, most reckless, and definitely the most suicidal thing I have ever done in my life.

I smacked that dragon right across the nose and yelled:

"I gave back your gold, you stupid dragon! So go find someone your own size to pick on!"

With a sharp intake of breath, Akar drew up to its full height. "No one hits Akar!"

"No one hits you," I said, feeling even more reckless. "No one takes your gold. Just what are people allowed to do around you, huh?"

"Die."

With that simple word, my new-found boldness deflated like a pricked balloon.

This was it. Akar was just one breath away from roasting me like a chicken. Or so I thought.

Leaping suddenly out of the darkness, Gavril tackled me and sent us both rolling across the uneven cave floor — just as the dragon let loose a blazing inferno.

Gavril then yanked me to my feet and hauled me behind a large rock. He stood there for a moment, sword in hand, surveying the situation.

"Thanks, Gavril. Your timing was perfect."

He gave me a brief smile. "As always."

That made me laugh. Yeah, it may have sounded like Gavril was boasting, but he did have a knack for showing up at just the right moment.

"Where's your torch?" I asked.

"Lost it. But don't worry. Akar is giving off plenty of light for us to see by."

True. The dragon was so furious it was

breathing out a bonfire.

"We need a shield," Gavril said. He looked over at the dragon's treasure trove. "You stay here. I'll be right back."

"But—"

Gavril darted out from the shelter of the rock and made a dash for the nook.

When the dragon saw him, it let loose another ball of fire.

"Gavril! Look out!"

With an impressive tuck and roll, Gavril dodged the flames. He skidded into the nook, sending coins scattering in all directions. He managed to grab a large shield just as the pursuing dragon sent another volley of flames his way.

Using the shield as, well, a shield, Gavril spun out of the nook, landed right in front of Akar, and struck with his sword.

"Yay, Gavril!" I cried, but the words died on my lips as I said them. The blade bounced off the dragon's scaly skin like it was made of rock.

Gavril backed toward me as the dragon continued to advance, thrusting again and again with his sword without even making a scratch.

As for Akar, the dragon seemed to be enjoying the game. It lowered its great head and roared out flames. It swung with its tail, trying to trip Gavril up. It batted at Gavril with its claws.

It was playing with Gavril like a cat might play with a mouse before it pounces on it and eats it.

Gavril glanced over his shoulder at me. "Tim, get over here!"

"What?!"

"Get behind me and the shield. Now!"

Oh yeah, it made perfect sense to put myself in the line of fire. Not! But it would have been no use to argue with him about it. So I took a deep breath, left the shelter of the rock, and darted behind Gavril.

"Good lad," he said. "Now stay close."

The dragon let out a roar with another burst of fire. It was probably thrilled to have another shot at me. But Gavril quickly blocked the flames with his oversized shield, and the game continued.

Step back two steps. Strike with the sword. Duck behind the shield to avoid flames. Step back again. Strike, strike. Dodge the massive claw. Strike, strike. Duck again.

You get the picture.

Before long, my eyes and throat were burning from the smoke, and my head was swimming from the heat of the flames. I didn't know how Gavril was holding up, but I wanted this party to be over.

"Not much farther!" he cried.

I glanced behind me and was surprised to see the low, narrow entrance to a tunnel not fifteen feet away. And lying next to it was what looked very much like Beriman's hat.

It was the tunnel. *The* tunnel that the others went through! And it was much too small for the dragon to enter. If I wasn't so busy dodging fireballs, I would have busted out into another happy dance.

We were going to escape!

But the dragon had other ideas. It gave a little snort, accompanied by a puff of fiery smoke. "It's time to end this. Now!"

Before the words were even out of its mouth, Akar whipped around its enormous tail and swept our feet out from under us.

I hit the rocky floor hard and rolled (fortunately) in the direction of the tunnel. I leapt up, yelling: "Come on, Gavril!"

Not getting a reply, I looked back — and was instantly horrified.

Gavril was lying right under the dragon. His sword was just spinning to a stop several feet away, and the shield was nowhere to be seen. They must have both flown from his hands as he fell.

The creature was leaning over him, its breath coming out of its mouth in a low flame.

"How would you like to die, Gavril of Tryton? Shall I cook you first or eat you raw?"

"No!" I cried, leaping forward. "Leave him alone!"

The dragon turned its massive head toward me. "Silence, little thief. I'll deal with you next."

Gavril reached his hand toward the long, slim sheath attached to his belt. "It's over, Akar!"

Pulling out his grandfather's famous jeweled dagger, he struck at the dragon's underbelly.

Akar bellowed and flew backwards, crashing into a large stalagmite about one hundred feet away.

I rushed over to Gavril. "Are you okay?"

Gavril pushed himself to his feet. "I didn't kill it."

I looked at the dragon. It had lifted one wing and was examining its belly. "Nope, it's still alive. Let's go, okay?"

Gavril didn't seem to hear me. "I don't understand. I was supposed to slay the dragon like my grandfather did. That's my destiny. That's why the knife was handed down to me."

At that point, I was barely paying attention to

him. The dragon had lowered its wing and was staring at us with fire in its eyes and flames on his breath.

I snatched up Gavril's sword and shoved it into his hand. "We need to go. Come on!"

Gavril still wasn't moving, so I grabbed his arm and began pulling him toward the tunnel.

At that same moment, Akar let loose another round of flames and launched into the air, shooting toward us like a fiery missile.

"Quick, Gavril! Into the tunnel!"

Gavril hesitated at the entrance, looking back.

The dragon was almost on top of us.

"Go! Go!" I screamed in that embarrassingly high voice I get when I'm really freaked out.

Gavril dove into the tunnel, and I scurried in after him, snatching up Beriman's hat on the way.

Behind us in the cavern, Akar let out a roar to end all roars, shaking the ground and showering down little bits of rock on us.

"The tunnel is collapsing!" I yelled.

"No, it's not," Gavril yelled back. "Keep moving."

I did as he said, grateful that Gavril was sounding a bit more like his old self.

A fiery blast from the dragon lit up the tunnel like a searchlight, which made the going easy for about five seconds.

Then, Akar's fire was spent and the "lights" went out.

Everything was black.

Pitch black.

And I swear I heard the dragon laugh.

Into the Light

Akar probably thought it was funny to leave us in the darkest dark I had ever seen (or not seen).

But I sure didn't.

We were stuck in a cramped little tunnel in pitch blackness. What if we stumbled into a bottomless pit? What if we were eaten alive by some hideous friend of the dragon that was hiding in the dark?

What if we never found our way out alive?

"Tim, are you okay?" Gavril asked. "You're breathing funny."

"Am I okay? Yeah, fine. I'm just having a little panic attack, that's all."

"What's the problem?"

Gavril couldn't see it in the dark, but my jaw dropped so low it bounced off the stone floor. "What's the problem? Hello! Can't you see the mess we're in? No, that's right. You CAN'T see! We're stuck in a dark tunnel *without a light!*"

"We'll never find our way out of here," I continued without even pausing for a breath. "We're going to die — that's what's going to happen. Not that you care. You would have been happy if the dragon roasted us both to a crisp back there!"

"Tim, that's not true!"

"Then why did I have to haul you out of there? We barely made it into the tunnel in time!"

"I wasn't supposed to retreat! I was supposed to kill the dragon!"

Okay...

"I failed," Gavril said, sounding like it was a new thing to him.

It probably was.

"I had my grandfather's knife," he continued. "I struck the dragon in the right spot, just like I've been taught. I should have killed him. How am I ever going to face my father again?"

"But you saved my life. And we got out of there in one piece. Doesn't that count?"

"Not to my father. It would have been far more valiant of me to die fighting the dragon."

I couldn't help but give a little laugh. "And I thought *my* family was messed up!"

Gavril gave a grunt. "Well, we still have a mission to accomplish. We must get the queen's mirror to my father. I dare not fail at doing *that*."

I frowned in the dark. "Small problem, Gavril. Last I saw, Ron gave the mirror to Kat. But I don't know how we're supposed to find her when we can't see our hands in front of our faces."

I could hear Gavril shifting his position. "We'll just have to move ahead slowly and feel our way at first. The closer we get to the others, the better we'll see. They still have torches, remember?"

"Yeah, but how do we know which way to go?"

"Straight ahead. See how the darkness is fainter up there? That indicates light in the area, which tells me the others are nearby."

I looked. "I don't see a thing. Are you lying to me to make me feel better?"

"Trust me. I told Beriman to wait for me at the

first bend in the tunnel. They'll be there, so let's go."

Gavril began to inch slowly forward, and I gave a little shrug and followed him. What else could I do? Sit there in the dark by myself?

Not an option.

Besides, Gavril was right (as always). As we crept cautiously down the tunnel, the darkness did lift a little. And it wasn't long before I started hearing voices.

"We need to go back for them!" (That was Ron.)

"It's too dangerous." (That sounded like Erick.)

"I'll go," a gruff-sounding voice said.

"No, Beriman," said the voice that was most definitely Erick. "You said Gavril told us to meet him here. Let's just give him and Timmy a few more minutes. Then, you and I can check on them."

"No, you need to go now! Timmy is probably being eaten alive at this very moment!" (That was Kat. She had no faith in me at all!)

While she was still speaking, we rounded a corner and saw the others ahead of us — huddled together in conversation in the light of two blazing torches.

"Kat's right," Ron said. "We've waited long enough. Someone has to go back for them now."

Gavril cleared his throat. "No need for that."

Four heads snapped toward us. Kat spoke first: "Gavril? Timmy?"

And then everyone rushed us like we were rock stars. I even got a hug from Kat, which was one for the record books.

She, of course, later denied it.

I returned Beriman's hat to him, and Gavril gave everyone a quick recap of our battle with Akar, ending with: "The dragon is still alive, I'm afraid. So we need to keep our eyes open until we're free of these caves."

"You didn't kill it?" asked Ron.

Something like a shadow passed over Gavril's face. "No, I didn't."

Kat frowned. "Why not?"

Gavril looked down, and I suddenly felt angry. I wasn't going to let him call himself a failure in front of Kat — or any of us.

"I don't know, Kat," I said. "Maybe you should have stuck around and fought the dragon for us, since you seem to know so much."

"What's your problem, Timmy? I was just asking."

Erick cleared his throat. "I think we'd better be moving on. Beriman, are you ready to get us out of here?"

Beriman gave his hat a quick adjustment and nodded. "Of course. I was just waiting for you people."

With Beriman leading us once again, we traveled on for hours. Mostly uphill. In some places, the going was so difficult that I had to climb up the rocks using my hands and feet and scoot down them on my butt.

We didn't see the dragon again — fortunately. But we burned through our torches like they were just plain matchsticks.

It was terrifying.

Listen, I had a taste of how dark those tunnels were without any light. And it traumatized me for life. I'm probably going to have to sleep with a night light on until I'm forty.

Anyway, what I'm trying to say is that the last thing I wanted — the absolute *last* thing — was to lose our light.

We were on our last torch — and I was considering having my second panic attack of the day — when I noticed something wonderful.

"Hey, the tunnel is becoming brighter!"

"We're almost out of here!" Ron said, high-fiving me.

"Take it easy, guys," Kat said. "It's probably just another false alarm."

"It is not."

But, the words were barely out of my mouth before I (grudgingly) realized she had a point. After all, whenever the tunnel grew steeper or the weird "cave breeze" got stronger, Ron and I always jumped to the conclusion that the exit was just a few steps away.

And we were always wrong.

But not this time.

Nope.

In fact, I was willing to bet my entire Star Wars action figure collection that this was the real deal.

I would have told Kat so, but we rounded a bend, and my response died on my lips.

Light.

Glorious light.

It was streaming in through a large opening cut into the stone not twenty feet away from us.

The exit.

I wanted to laugh. I wanted to cry. I wanted to jump up and down.

Daylight! I was right!

I couldn't wait to get out of that dark tunnel. I broke into a run and plowed right into the arm Gavril put out to stop me.

"Hold up, Tim."

"But Gavril! I want out of here!"

"We don't know what's out there. Let me go first and make sure it's safe."

Erick stepped in front of him. "No way, Gavril. We can't risk losing you."

Gavril stared at him. "Now you're being ridiculous."

"He is not, my prince," Beriman said. "I happen to agree with him."

"I do, too," Kat said.

Gavril threw up his hands. "Fine. You go first, Erick. Just take care."

"Oh, I will. I have no desire to be captured and thrown back into the queen's dungeon."

Flashing us a reassuring grin, Erick approached the opening slowly. He paused just inside the cave, shielding his eyes from the sunlight as he peered out. Then, he stepped out into the brightness and disappeared from our sight.

I held my breath. The minutes ticked past. No Erick.

"Where is he?"

"Patience, Tim," Gavril said. "He's taking a look around like I told him to."

"But what if he's been captured by the queen's men? What if they're waiting right outside the tunnel for us?"

"What if you're being an idiot?" Kat said.

"What if you're being annoying?"

I could see Kat glaring at me in the dim light. "What if you are?"

"What if *you* are?"

Gavril rolled his eyes. (Yes, it was light enough for me see it.) "What if you both just be quiet?"

Erick chose that moment to appear again in the opening and waved us on.

I dropped my argument with Kat and ran forward — and this time Gavril didn't hold me back. I bolted out into the sunlight and came to a sudden stop.

Ron promptly ran into me. Again.

Why was he always doing that?

"Sorry, Timmy. I didn't see you. It's so bright out here. My eyes haven't adjusted from the tunnels yet."

Mine hadn't either, which was why I stopped in the first place. But I got my "daylight eyes" back pretty fast, and I just couldn't stop looking around.

The sunshine was a mellow, golden color. It shone down around us, turning the leaves overhead and the brambles underneath the most brilliant shades of green. Everything looked so bright and fresh.

Kat turned her face up to the sun and spread out her arms. "Ah... I can finally get warm. I was so cold in those tunnels."

I was, too, but I wasn't about to admit it. I'm a guy, after all — not a wimpy girl like my sister.

"It's late afternoon," Gavril said. "We need to press on for the castle while we still have light."

I sat up from where I had sprawled out on a soft, spongy patch of grass. "Already? Can't we have a few minutes, Gavril? We've been stuck in those dark, damp tunnels for like forever."

Beriman scoffed. "They weren't that damp. Besides, we weren't even in those tunnels for a full two days."

"Well, it felt like forever," I said, lying back on the grass again.

Erick stretched lazily. "Yeah, what's a few extra minutes, Gavril?"

Gavril sighed. "Erick, I thought you of all people would realize—"

"IIIIIIIIIEEEEEEEEEEEEEEEEEEE!"

Gavril stopped in mid-sentence. Erick bolted upright. And I nearly jumped out of my skin.

That was Kat. Screaming. And pointing up the hill into the bushes.

Gavril was instantly at her side. "What is it?"

"A galrog," she whispered hoarsely. "It's one of those galrog things."

I followed her pointing finger — and gulped. Yep, it was a galrog all right.

Instantly, everyone drew their swords.

Well, everyone except Kat and me. Kat didn't have one to draw, and I was trying hard to forget I had a weapon hanging at my side.

I wasn't exactly eager to face one of those things again.

Ever.

Gavril led the charge up the hill, but the galrog didn't wait around. It turned and ran, disappearing behind a large rock.

"It's getting away!" I cried, pointing.

Gavril stopped and scanned the hillside. "It's no use," he finally told the others. "We'll never catch it now."

They had barely picked their way back down the hill before Kat pounced:

"What was that thing doing here?"

"I'll bet it was waiting for us," I said, feeling braver now that I knew the galrog had gone.

Kat frowned. "Timmy, that's stupid. Why would it do that?"

I opened my mouth to respond, but Erick beat me to it:

"No, that makes sense. The queen knew we had entered the mountain. And she knows where we would come out. So she sent the galrog ahead to watch for us—"

"And alert her when we appeared," Gavril said, finishing his sentence for him.

We looked at each other for a moment. I could hear the birds chirping away in the trees. A bee buzzed by like a wobbly bullet.

When Gavril broke the silence, he did nothing to lift the mood. "If Queen Morissa drove the soldiers with few breaks, then she's not far behind us. We need to move out now and march through the night if we're going to reach the castle before she does."

March through the night?

My mouth dropped open. "Are you kidding me?"

Gavril turned and looked at me.

And then I remembered. He never kids.

Outnumbered

We pressed on through the night, just as Gavril promised, stumbling over unseen tree roots (that would mostly be me), dodging (not always successfully) low-hanging branches, and getting tangled up in prickly bushes (me again).

And whenever we wanted to stop — whenever we just felt too tired to take another step — Gavril would urge us on.

Yep, you guessed it. We didn't get one wink of sleep. Not even a half a wink. I told you before that Gavril is brutal. It's like he's a cyborg or something. (I have my suspicions.)

Of course, the whole time I was "bulldozing" my way through the woods — Kat's word, not mine — I kept looking over my shoulder and straining my ears for any sign of pursuit. Not that I could really *see* anything in the dark, of course, or *hear* anything over the noise we were making.

That's right. With the exception of Gavril, whom I'm convinced walks on air, we sounded like a bunch of clumsy, overweight bears being chased through the woods by a swarm of angry bees.

Yes, even Kat.

By the time daylight finally arrived, I was tired all the way down to my bones and hungry enough to eat a plateful of slugs.

If I didn't get a break soon — and scarf down whatever deer jerky we had left in our packs — I was going to pitch my biggest fit since that meltdown I had in Walmart when I was two. (I don't remember it, but I heard it was epic.)

I gave a loud sigh. "Are we almost there?"

Gavril turned his head to answer me. "Not much farther, Tim. The castle is just around —"

He broke off, his eyes widening. "Soldiers! Run!"

What?!

I looked back. Sure enough, I could see the queen's men marching through the forest. It was hard to tell from that distance, but I could swear they didn't look as nearly as hungry or as tired as I felt.

Fortunately, fear kicked in, and I ran.

"I thought going through those tunnels was supposed to get us way ahead of the queen's army," Ron said while running.

"I was hoping it would," Gavril said, answering without slowing his pace. "But I warned you that the queen might have driven her men to march nonstop, which, obviously, they did."

"Nonstop?" Kat asked breathlessly. "But that's impossible."

"Not if they're cyborgs," I said just as breathlessly.

Yeah, my cyborg theory had been extended to include *everyone* in that land. They were all so good at physical stuff — like marching and fighting — that it was almost inhuman. It seemed like a logical explanation to me, but Kat didn't agree.

"Timmy, that's just stupid."

"No it isn't."

"Yes, it is!"

"They're *not* cyborgs!" Erick said. "Stop arguing and run faster, you two!"

We rounded a bend in the trail and shot out into a large, open field. I could see the castle on the other side — the water of its moat shimmering in the sun like liquid diamonds. All we had to do was make it across the field, and we would be safe. There only one problem.

"The drawbridge is up!" I said. "How are we supposed to get inside?"

Gavril skidded to a halt, sending clumps of grass flying. "Tim, quick. Give your sword to Kat."

"Why?" I asked, pulling it out of my sheath and reluctantly handing it to her. "I can fight, too, you know."

Beriman made a noise that must have been a cough and NOT a laugh. Surely, he didn't laugh.

Gavril's lips twitched — like he was trying not to smile.

Or laugh.

I looked down to study my now filthy Nikes. "Well, I can, you know."

Gavril cleared his throat. "Sure you can, Tim. But I need you to do something else."

He shoved the mirror into my hands. "Take this and run for the castle. One of the guards will see you approaching and will lower the drawbridge. Get the mirror to the king."

"But what if I can't find him?"

"Then smash the mirror on Dragon Rock. It must be destroyed."

Kat was shaking her head. "No, it's too dangerous. Let me take the mirror instead of Timmy.

I can run faster than him."

"No, Tim takes the mirror." Gavril glanced back into the woods and then looked at me with even more intensity than usual, which is saying a lot. He gave me a shove. "Go, go!"

I took off like the Road Runner being chased by Wile E. Coyote in that old *Looney Tunes* show. But I didn't get far before I heard Kat scream.

Wheeling to a stop, I looked behind me.

The queen's army was pouring out of the forest and into the clearing — and they outnumbered us about a bazillion to one.

But Gavril didn't even hesitate for a second. He raised his sword and launched himself at the nearest soldier, who just happened to be that nasty Seaton.

I couldn't help but cheer. I really didn't like that guy.

Meanwhile, Erick struck at another man, showing off some serious sword-fighting skills I never dreamed he had. And Beriman got busy charging a much taller dude, using his short sword to drive the man back into the woods.

That left about fifty guys (yeah, I exaggerated earlier) that were looking for some action. And their eyes were on Ron and Kat.

"Look out!" I yelled, as a guy shaped like the Pillsbury Doughboy lunged at my brother.

Ron swung around and blocked the man's blade with his sword. The soldier looked surprised, but he got over it in about a second and lit into Ron with a flurry of sword strikes.

"Ron!" Kat screamed.

At first, I thought she was concerned about Ron. (I know I was.) But no. A skinny soldier with Hitler's mustache was taking swipes at her!

"A little busy here," Ron said to her, quickly side-stepping to avoid being skewered by Captain Doughboy.

Kat was swinging her sword, trying to block Mustache Guy's blows. But honestly? She was fighting like a girl, and she didn't stand a chance against him. (Don't tell her I said that.)

I found myself running toward them. I wasn't thinking about Gavril's command to get the mirror to the king. I wasn't thinking about not having a sword, although I probably should have been.

I actually don't think I was thinking at all. My brother and sister were in danger. I needed to help them. What was there to think about?

"Tim!"

At the tone of Gavril's voice, I slid to a stop.

"Get that mirror to the king. Now!" he said. And then he leapt in between Kat and Mr. Hitler-Mustache with his sword flying.

I was about to obey him — really, I was — but the queen chose that moment to step out of the shadows of the forest.

And I was instantly distracted.

How could I not be? The sun was shining on her like a spotlight, making the gold trim on her dress sparkle and her hair blaze like fire.

I know I'm only twelve, but I couldn't help but notice how beautiful she looked.

Too bad she's so evil.

While I was watching, the queen threw her arms dramatically up in the air and (just as dramatically) said:

"Get the mirror! The man who returns it to me

will be rewarded beyond his wildest dreams with up to half of my kingdom!"

The soldiers who weren't busy fighting looked around. And that's when everything really went downhill.

"Look!" a dude with a crooked nose said, pointing at me. "The boy! He's got the mirror!"

Uh-oh!

"Timmy, run!" Kat screamed.

Battle for the Mirror

My sister's command was totally unnecessary. I was already running like a rabbit spotted by a pack of hounds.

I had a good head start, but the heavy mirror slowed me down. And it wasn't long before I had a bunch of sweaty, smelly soldiers breathing down my neck.

A hand grabbed my arm and jerked me around.

Seaton! I thought Gavril had taken care of him.

Guess not.

He smiled, flashing those yellow, crooked teeth again. The guy seriously needed to see a dentist.

"Hand over the mirror, little runt," he said.

Runt? That got my attention away from his teeth. Did he really call me a runt?

Seaton raised his sword and started tickling my collarbone with it. "Didn't you hear me, runt?"

There it was again. I felt my jaw stiffen. No one calls me a runt. Well, except for my brother and sister, but I've gotten used to that.

"I'm going to count to three," Seaton continued. "If you don't give me the mirror by the time I'm done, you will die."

I glared at him. "You should try counting to ten. Or don't you know how?"

Yeah, I know. Dumb. But the jerk did just call me

a runt. Twice. And the words came out before I could stop them.

Seaton pressed the tip of his sword against my skin.

Ouch. I swear he drew blood.

"You're lucky I don't kill you now," he said and began to count. "One..."

I quickly glanced around for Gavril, Erick, or someone. "A little help here," I called.

"Two..."

I got louder. "Help!"

"Three!"

Seaton raised his sword, and I flinched back, holding up the mirror like a shield and hoping for the best.

What else could I do? No weapon, remember?

Suddenly, a blurred shape burst between me and Seaton — almost knocking me off my feet.

Ron!

My brother stood in front of Seaton, sword in hand. He gave me a quick glance. "You okay?"

"Just peachy."

"Stay behind me." Ron turned to Seaton. "You want the mirror? Then you gotta go through me."

"Gladly."

Seaton struck at him with his sword. Ron fought back, but it quickly became obvious that Seaton was a master swordsman and my brother was not.

To be fair, Ron was pretty good. But he had only learned to sword fight like two days ago. All it took was a quick flip of Seaton's wrist to send his sword sailing out of his hand.

Great.

The soldiers around us cheered. A few of them

even laughed.

Ron's face got red. Some people might have thought he was embarrassed. But I know my brother.

He was ticked off.

Seaton aimed his blade at Ron's chest and said: "I win. Tell the runt to hand over the mirror."

"You're going down."

Ron's voice was so low that only Seaton and I could hear it.

Seaton took a half step back, the tips of his ears glowing bright pink. "What?"

"You're. Going. Down."

With a roar, Ron ducked under Seaton's sword, plowed into his midsection, and took him down to the ground with a bone-crunching thud.

The guy never saw it coming. In a matter of half a second, he was laid out in the grass — apparently unconscious.

(I said "apparently" because I was convinced the wimp was faking it.)

Ron leapt to his feet and quickly stooped to retrieve his sword.

"That was amazing," I said to him. "How did you—"

"Later, Timmy. Right now, you might want to duck."

Huh?

I ducked, and Ron's sword sliced through the air over my head and met against another blade with a loud clank.

"Go!" he yelled.

Adrenaline surging, I took off toward the castle and ran right into the heat of the battle. I paused, trying to figure out how I was going to get through the fighting without being skewered like a shish kabob.

"Look out!" Gavril yelled.

Out of the corner of my eye, I saw a flash near my right shoulder. I dodged to the left and narrowly missed losing an ear. Gavril blocked the guy's next blow with his sword, and I left them to duke it out.

But I only managed to get another ten feet or so before another soldier took a swipe at me.

Yeesh!

Luckily for me, Erick leapt in with his mad sword skills before the guy could take another poke at me. But come on! How was I supposed to get the mirror to the king when everyone kept gunning for me?

I dropped to the ground to avoid another sword strike and started to crawl. It was no small feat to get through the fighting on my hands and knees while dragging along a mirror, but it was worth a shot. If people didn't see me, maybe they wouldn't kill me.

My plan worked out great — until I crawled headfirst into a pair of solid (and immovable) legs. With a sinking feeling, I looked up and saw a set of crooked, yellow teeth grinning down at me.

Yeah, you guessed it...

Seaton.

He was supposed to be unconscious. (I told you he was faking it!)

The jerk pointed his sword at me and said, "Hand over the mirror."

No surprises there. I slowly got to my feet, clutching the mirror to my chest and doing my best to avoid the sharp end of his sword. Glancing around, I could see that all my friends were busy fighting — even Kat, who was holding her sword with both hands and swinging it like an ax.

(Yeah, I know. It was a miracle she was still alive.)

None of them noticed that I was in trouble. None of them realized that I was about to lose the mirror to Mr. Nasty Teeth.

The thought of it made me feel sick. I couldn't look at Seaton's sneering, gloating face. So instead, I gazed past his right ear at the castle and got the surprise of my life.

The drawbridge was down. And pouring over it were dozens of the king's soldiers!

They let out a roar as they charged, and I found myself yelling and jumping up and down — much like Ron did when the New England Patriots won the Super Bowl.

As for Seaton, his expression went from puzzlement over my behavior to sheer terror as the king's men joined the battle.

It was awesome.

Even better, he quickly became too busy fighting to worry about me, so I was able to get back to my mission: Getting the mirror to the king.

I pushed my way through the battling soldiers and there he was. The Main Man. The Head Honcho. The Big Cheese.

Yeah, I'm talking about King Gunther. He was standing at the end of the drawbridge. And judging by the smile on his face, he was happy to see me.

"Young Tim," he said. "Hurry. Bring the mirror here."

I trotted toward the king, feeling like a hero. Well, I kind of was. Me. Tim Hunter. I was the one who got the mirror to the king. Who's the man now, huh?

I was so lost in my thoughts — wondering if there would be a reward for my efforts (or maybe a parade in my honor) — that I didn't pay attention to the blur of green I saw out of the corner of my eye.

And then it was too late.

A terrific force slammed into me, knocking me right off my feet. The mirror flew out of my hands, and I hit the ground so hard it took my breath away.

I lay there for a moment, stunned. I shook my head to clear it and tried to move, but a heavy weight was on top of me, pinning me down.

What in the world?

And then I heard a laugh, right next to my ear.

I knew that laugh. I heard it for the first time when I was thrown into the dungeon — and it will haunt my nightmares for years to come.

It belonged to the queen.

My face flushed hot. I was tackled by the queen! A girl! How embarrassing is that?

Instantly, I thought of the mirror. It was lying just a few yards away from me — free of the velvet wrap and glittering in the sun. I needed to get to it before the queen did, or everything was lost.

I felt the queen tense and spring away from me. She was going for the mirror!

With a quick thrust of my hands against the springy grass, I launched myself after her and managed to grab ahold of one of her legs.

"Oh no, you don't!" I yelled.

Whack!

Queen Morissa kicked with her free leg, clocking me on my jaw and loosening my hold.

Ouch!

Face throbbing, I pushed myself up to my knees, but it was too late. The queen was scrambling forward now — her outstretched hand mere inches from the mirror.

I hung my head. I couldn't bear to watch her win. Not after everything we had been through.

Suddenly, a horrible cry pierced the air. "NO!"

My head jerked up, and my eyes couldn't believe what they were seeing.

King Gunther was standing over the queen. And in his hands was the mirror.

Silence fell upon the clearing. I was vaguely aware that the soldiers had stopped fighting, but I was too focused on what was happening with the mirror to pay them much attention.

"Give that to me," Queen Morissa hissed, grabbing at the mirror from a kneeling position.

The king was looking at his reflection in the glass.

Wait... he wasn't supposed to do that, was he? The mirror could bewitch him, and he could become power-hungry like the queen!

I opened my mouth to say something, but stopped. The king had pulled his eyes away from the mirror and was smiling. Maybe everything was okay.

He looked down at the queen, and an expression of what might have been pity crossed his face.

"Sorry, my dear," he said. Then he turned and walked slowly toward the castle with the mirror.

The kings' soldiers cheered.

"No!" The queen seemed to wilt right there on the grass. I kind of felt sorry for her.

Nah, not really!

I felt a hand on my back.

"Nice work, Tim," Gavril said, helping me to my feet. "I knew I could count on you."

The others crowded around us. Ron. Kat. Erick. Beriman. They were all there. They all had survived the battle.

My eyes felt wet, but I wasn't crying. I don't cry. I was just really happy everyone was still alive.

"It's over, right?" Ron said. "The king has the mirror. We can go home."

"Yes," Erick said, clapping him on the back. "It's over. I'm so proud of all of you. Weren't they amazing, Gavril?"

"Uh, yes," Gavril said, pulling his eyes away from the castle.

He had been watching the king go through the castle gate. How did I know? I was watching him, too.

"I'm sorry," Gavril said. "I have to excuse myself to speak with my father. Please don't go home without saying goodbye."

"Why? Is something wrong?" I asked.

Gavril hesitated. "Hopefully not. I just want to make sure he destroys the mirror."

"We'll go with you," Erick said. "We have to pass right by Dragon Rock to get to the other mirror anyway. The one that will take us home."

Home.

I shook off my little, niggling worries and gave a grin as I followed the others toward the castle.

We were going home!

My heart soared. I was going to see my mom again! And I was going to eat pepperoni pizza, burgers and French fries until I got sick!

It was going to be great!

I was so happy that I practically skipped my way through the castle gate and into the courtyard. I could see King Gunther standing by Dragon Rock, right where he was supposed to be.

But he was staring into the mirror again.

My feet slowed.

The king glanced up, and his eyes met mine.

My heart sank.

That's when I knew...

Something was terribly wrong.

Don't Close the Book Yet!

First, THANK YOU for reading *The Mirror of Doom!*

If you liked it, please tell your friends. Even better, leave a review! You don't have to even write much. Just one word — like "Awesome!" — would be fine. (But only if you thought it was awesome!)

Second, click on the link below to sign up for my email list. That way... you can be the first to hear when the next book of my adventures comes out. (It may or may not involve some nasty, smelly giants, but that's all I'm going to say!) PLUS, you'll get a cool FREE gift!

Yep, I'll send you an e-book copy of the "missing chapter" from *The Mirror of Doom* — called *Saving Tim Hunter* — totally free!

Did you wonder how Gavril and Erick managed to sneak into the queen's castle, overpower the guards, and rescue me from the locked tower?

I did, too! So I bugged Gavril until he told me the story.

You can get the e-book version of this "missing chapter" here:

http://mirrorofdoom.com/get-missing-chapter/

Just enter your email and it's yours - for free!

Here We All Are!

Myself

Kat

Ron

Gavril

Beriman

Erick

Uncle Edgar

Gunther

Morissa

Akar

Bailey Baxter is the pen name of a somewhat successful copywriter who writes online "junk mail" for health supplement companies. (Trust me... she'd rather be writing books.) She lives in Asheville, NC with a mischievous Shih-tzu named Lucy and a pantry full of chocolate. Dark chocolate. This is her debut children's novel.

LaSablonnière has been drawing pictures since he was old enough to hold a pencil. When he's illustrating children's books, he goes by just one name - like Madonna. This secretive artist also works as a web designer - and talks about *Star Wars* more than any human being I know. He lives with his wife, two kids, and faithful dog Chloe in Willington, CT.

CPSIA information can be obtained
at www.ICGtesting.com
Printed in the USA
LVOW03s1500211117
557190LV00012B/613/P